THE BOOK OF STAN

DAVID EWALD

The author would like to thank Valerie Sayers, Michael Lidbetter, Kieran Kennedy, William O'Rourke, and Jervey Tervalon for their invaluable assistance with early drafts of this novel.

Excerpts from "The Thunder, Perfect Mind," translated by George W. MacRae, 1979, Brill Publishers. Used by permission.

for Karen and for Jeffrey

ONE

I sing a song for my sister, who used to be my brother, who sings a song for me.

I WANDER through darkness under the eye of the sun, a sinner without sin, a Man purified and tainted, blasphemous and blest, reverent and profane, alone and befriended.

I GO door to door campaigning for The Savior, he who will unite our country. October now, cobwebs on cacti, the crunch of rocks underneath my combat boots. I hold The Book and nothing else. The Book is all I need. That and my smile. And the promise of The List.

"I'm not interested," the young pregnant woman, so like a Social star, so like her kind, says in the doorway.

"Hear me out," I say.

"Sorry," she says, and the door takes her place.

In that terrifying moment of being shut out—again—I think of stomping, like a Man should, in the space about to be closed off. My boot a doorjamb. I hesitate a moment too long, and the door slams, followed by the sound of a driven deadbolt.

I am fearful and I am to be feared.

I am so much stronger and I am still weak.

Perhaps if I told the young pregnant woman about Jeremy, Jer, Jeri, she would understand why I campaign for the man she will vote for in November. Perhaps if I explained what brought me here to The Valley, a new valley I have made my home, she would not be affronted by my rangy frame, my cracking smile, my unkempt beard, the scraggly hair that falls to my shoulders. She would not be affronted by my combat fatigues and boots, nor would she be affronted by my words. She would not be affronted by The Book. She would see that I am not packing anything but Peace—Peace between the sexes, Peace between our country's two sides. She would see what I have seen, felt what I have felt, and she would understand.

UNDERSTAND THIS: A month after the Supreme Court handed down its decision in *Obergefell vs. Hodges*, Jeremy and I hiked out to the Devil's Punchbowl. It was my idea, and my brother followed. Across the horizon the sun broke like a promise as I revved up my new truck and tore off through the San Diego Country Gems. At the Chaparral Falls trailhead on Rushing Road, I set the parking brake and put up the reflective visor. Before I could exit, my brother placed a hand on my arm.

"Let this be the end of it," he said.

"It will be," I affirmed.

Jer looked me in the eyes for the first time since we'd met days earlier at San Diego International. His smile failed to reveal his teeth. I felt his hand—his big forceful hand. My hand. As if daring me to withdraw my arm. As if he knew.

I brought my phone out. My brother did the same. Several notifications alerted me to the attention generated by my latest post on all my channels, originated on my site *From Adam*. The comments were coming in, my followers pleased as pugilists. I'd written again about the '90s, that glorious decade when the president got head in the White House, Baywatch dominated the screen, no Hooters employees dared file a lawsuit, and women didn't question the Victoria's Secret clothing line. Two decades later, much of that glory had faded if not altogether vanished. In 2015, men had the right to swim against these shifting currents. We would not be dragged out to sea, a one-way ticket on the Tahiti Express. We're not pigs, I wrote. We're Americans exercising our right to free speech. In this country we can say whatever we want, and those who don't like our views can tune us out at their peril.

As usual, several comments came from the knee-jerk reactionaries, the Eves, those touchy-feely sad-sacks who always read into my writing, found some sinister hidden meaning, a call to arms, a threat of—get this—*domestic terrorism*. Stan Pangborn, a domestic terrorist! I meant no such thing. And what if I did? Would it matter? The likes, the shares, the views kept increasing. I write lies and the truth. That's all that matters.

Jeremy smiled at his screen. Something from Eric, no doubt.

I knew no one.

He smiled as if he knew.

—*They*, Stan.

Not now. Okay?

—My *pronoun*...

Enough.

—Don't you know: I am the bride and the bridegroom.

Not that again.

—And it is my husband who begot me.

Whatever.

—See, brother: two can play your game.

It's no game. It's—

Jeremy abruptly threw open his door and exited my truck. He retrieved his backpack and slung it over one shoulder. For a time I kept him in the rearview mirror. He could have left without me. He didn't need me. We'd been ready to part ways our entire life.

The volunteer at the trailhead checked our permit. "You're the first," she said. "Maybe the only. You sure you want to be out there? It's supposed to get close to a hundred today."

"No sweat," I assured her.

"We'll be back before we fry," Jeremy added.

The volunteer nodded and waved us on. When we were at an acceptable distance, Jeremy said, in a low voice, "Annoying."

"Her lack of faith in us?"

"The fact that we have to even have a permit now."

"A kid died, Jer. Four years ago..."

"But to pay now.... Remember when there was no one, when we went alone together?"

"I'll always remember," I said.

"With any luck," Jer said, "the heat'll keep everyone away."

Twenty minutes in and the sun was beating down hard. We did not stop and turn back but marched ahead, as if we were kids again. The valley wide and vacant with the remnants of recent wildfires I found beguiling, beautiful, the way the earth's scars recalled the blackened bushes and fallen trees of our youth. When we were young, we were all too impressionable—and I had stayed so. Another fire will sweep through soon, I thought. Redeemed in The Valley of the Cleansed. We both will be forgiven.

We were 36 years old and minutes apart. Jeremy stood six-two and weighed a little over 200 pounds. His transitioning had caused him to gain weight since I'd last seen him. His body was changing. I had last seen him with his hair grown out and his fingernails long, but now I noticed his walk was different, he carried himself as if he'd been born into a new body and was just beginning to take comfort and achieve confidence. Most conspicuous of all—to me, to anyone who cared to notice—were the dual points rising through his shirt. Her shirt.

—*Their* shirt, Stan. *Their.*

I'm not going to try to understand this now.

—You never will.

I will. I've started.

—The Church of the Manifested is nowhere near "getting started."

Don't bring The Church into this. I'm trying to tell this the way it should be told.

—Sure you are.

Let me tell this story, damnit.

—Have at it.

I assumed the therapy was working. We were splitting in appearance, no longer identical.

—Am I going to have to set your story straight?

Silence accompanied us—

—Go ahead, Stanley. Ignore me.

—and I was beginning to suspect. My brother's mind might not have been entirely preoccupied with the high court's decision that he and Eric had been anticipating for months, years. The decision they'd known would fall in their favor.

—*He* and Eric? The truth, brother. Only the—

"I agree the permit sucks," I said. "No climbing anymore, no jumping..."

"But Stan...the kid who died, *remember*?"

"One death out of how many people jumping? Diving? Falling? In how many decades?"

"That we know of," my brother, my sister, said. "It's gotta be called the Devil's Punchbowl for some reason."

Jeremy's arm shot out across my stomach and held me back. I looked up and saw farther ahead what would have been my death: a rattlesnake crossing the baked and cracked trail in no hurry. Under my breath I thanked my brother, my sister. We waited, the heat rising through my Cowboys cap. This wait will be worth it, I said. Not my death.

A little over an hour later, with the sun in full force, we reached the trail's end: the Devil's Punchbowl, known officially as Chaparral Falls. I had chosen a Thursday on purpose, hoping there would be at most only a few hikers present at the nearly dry natural basin, but Invincible Father smiled on me this morning: no one was in sight. Jeremy caught me grinning.

"You're really thinking of jumping, aren't you?"

"Maybe."

"They'll fine you for that."

"Government takes even more of my money. What's new? I don't see anyone watching me. Unless you're going to snitch…"

"Who, me?" Jer said, taken aback I would even think of him (her) that way. "You do you, bro."

"We'll do it together."

"I'm not climbing with you."

"Like when we were kids. Together. Unless you've changed…"

Jeremy took a moment. At last he raised his eyes to stare me down. "I haven't changed," he said. "Let's go."

Despite this being the end of July and the start of another brutal round of heat, the Punchbowl wasn't as dry as I'd expected. Though low, the water level was tolerable for swimming, the surface dark and rippling. Jer and I scrambled over boulders, smoother and smoother as we neared the natural pool. Reaching the edge, we gazed into the water. Jer touched my back. I allowed this, though I wouldn't look at him, her. My line of vision widened to take in the top of the waterfall, a trickle flowing down the cliff face. When we were kids, the cliff was not as slanted, not as much of a chute carrying the water into the basin. Years and years of natural erosion as well as daredevil buffoonery from those interested in partying instead of preserving nature had turned the attraction into a towering slide. That wouldn't be the way to go, I thought.

"We're going to the top," I announced.

"The very top. That's like a hundred feet."

"I've never been all the way up there."

"There's a reason for that, you know."

"Jer..."

"What?"

"I wish you'd show me..."

"That I can be like you?" Jeremy said. "Someone you'll approve of?"

"I didn't say that."

"You're right. What am I saying? You don't even approve of yourself."

"All right. We won't go up."

"Oh no," Jer said. "After all this hot fuss I'm not chickening out. Let's go. Just watch my back. If rocks start to give out anywhere, let me know, okay?"

We left the pool for the side of the cliff face. A tenuous path had been carved out long before. Stones formed steps our feet took with caution. I heaved and puffed as I grasped rock after rock, tested each to make certain it would not come loose, and pulled myself up farther. My brother's, my sister's, rear end was the last thing I wanted to see as I ascended, but it had to be if I was to succeed. He, she, had to go first.

Jeremy gestured to a smooth flat outcrop jutting over the natural pool some distance below. "Last chance, Stanley."

"Heights were never your thing."

"They weren't yours either. I'm surprised you're such a jack rabbit with this."

"I'm driven," I said, and I

—I know all the awful thoughts you're driven by. *Almost* all the awful thoughts.

grasped what looked to be solid support. Instead the rock came loose, I could feel my body pulling back and away, and if I were to fall and even injure myself my mission would fail. I would not miss that flight.

The self-styled video game king of Gordon Lawrence Elementary saved himself that July morning; all that thumbing around on the controllers, developing hand-to-eye coordination, paid off. My free hand dropped the rock and, within the span of a second, had clung—granted, with just my fingertips —to a new, blessedly stable handhold.

My brother, my sister, asked if I still wanted to continue.

"Now more than ever. I've never seen the entire valley. You know this is our last time here."

—You remember how his hand felt—

Shut up. Shut. Up. Just give me your hand already.

With my brother's (sister's) support I flopped on level ground. Now the sun's stroke was inescapable, we were splayed out, ready for the roasting.

"Have to eat quick," Jeremy said.

"Just give me a moment," I wheezed.

Together we stood on top of the Devil's Punchbowl, the valley spread out before us, the mountains on the horizon stretching like a giant's toes.

To our immediate left, water flowed in a weak stream to the edge of the cliff and then cascaded over. I didn't want to venture close to the edge, but I had to. Just a glance. Forgetting my guard for a moment, forgetting what my brother (my sister) could do to me just as I would do to him (to her), I stepped forward on ginger feet and peered far, far down into the basin. Over a hundred foot drop. Still no one on the rocks below. No one paddling around in the natural pool. No one to watch us.

A woman's voice pierced the quiet. "Hold it right there!"

At the sound I scrambled—and nearly went over the edge. I turned to see my brother, my sister, cackling wildly.

"Got you, Stan."

"I should've known that was you."

I passed my brother, my sister, by and knelt for my back-pack. He, she—

—*They*.

She approached the edge. And I thought, watching her, watching him, this will see me through halfalife, as I come not with a sword but with a screen.

THE DOORBELL RANG, just as I knew it would. Opening up, I was confronted with two missionaries, Brannigan and Raybury, members of Madeline's church, the Church of the Manifested.

"You wanted to see us," Brannigan said. He was 21 or 22 at most, tall with blond hair, oil well eyes and a brawny build. His mouth made a small sucking sound. Raybury, his companion, younger, shorter, slighter with close-cropped dark hair and a narrow acne-ridden face, offered up a wan smile and a hello of sorts. Both young men were dressed alike: short-sleeved dark blue dress shirts, beige slacks and brown dress shoes. Their name tags were pinned across their hearts. Under-neath each name was etched the acronym CotM.

Brannigan stared at me hard before squinting his deep eyes, as if trapping a particle with his lids, and then his eyes snapped open, the light let in by God, and those coolly observant eyes drew me in, made me regret and hope anew. Raybury turned his attention to the American flag welcome mat and, like a child who's been reprimanded but still wants his way, prodded the mat with the toe of his spotless shoe. The missionaries remained on the threshold.

I invited them in. It had to be quick so I wouldn't have time to reconsider my plan. Once they were inside I showed them through the economy-sized kitchen, the darkened living room that most days managed to avoid the sun, the dining room with its large table at which Simone and I so often ate in silence while the imposing TV spoke for us. The TV was again speaking that afternoon, men around a fetus-shaped desk predicting outcomes in the next day's UFC Fight Night. Machida versus Romero. My money was on Romero. I left the TV on but muted the drum and the fife. Looking around, taking in the TV, the missionaries expressed appropriate approval and awe, compounded when they entered my bedroom at back. Here they saw my king-size bed in the corner, the movie posters (*Taxi Driver*, *The Godfather*, *Swingers*, *Gladiator*) tacked to the walls, above the bed the wide bay window looking out on the ocean. The open slider allowed a breeze into the room. The partially blinded sun played and danced on the mattress like leaves in autumn. I watched these alternating shards of light for a time, lulled by a memory of a vast and warm lawn, a sunflower's shadow stretched across the grass.

"You're the only one living here?" Raybury asked.

"Most nights I'm not alone," I said, "but, yes, this is my place and only mine. It's what happens when you work your way up in the ranks at a profitable company."

"What's your job?"

"My career," I said, "is marketing manager. Wasn't easy getting to that position…"

"I'm sure."

"But I stuck it out, and now I make bank."

"Sorry to point this out," Brannigan said, "but it's important for moving forward. You look like you're in your thirties."

"I'm about to turn 36."

"And you're not married, from the looks of it."

"No ring," Raybury added.

"I will be," I said. "That's in the works."

"What's her name?"

"Simone," I answered. "She's gorgeous, of course. Obviously wife material."

"I'm sure," Brannigan said for a second time. "I can picture her now."

"Can you," I said, wary.

"Yes," Brannigan said, and he closed his eyes.

Raybury closed his eyes as well.

"Guys," I said. "You can see her online. She has social media."

"Invincible Father prefers this method," Raybury admitted.

"Okay..." I said, and when I could stand the sight no longer I asked them into the living room, where they set their backpacks down and unzipped them. Brannigan brought out a large black book, thicker than any bible I'd seen. He strummed his fingers on the book's cover. I handed glasses of water over to the young men, who took nursing sips. Raybury opened his black book to a predetermined page, then ran his finger down the lines, muttering a new movement, the next phrase, his lizard-like tongue (to match his lizard-like countenance) darting out between his sharp teeth. His fingers were quick and hairless.

"That's not the Bible, is it."

"It's the Book of the Manifested," said Brannigan. "Everything we need is here. And if you're serious about this, Stan, if you're serious about discovering your path to ultimate fulfillment—"

"Ultimate pleasure," Raybury cut in.

"To Manifestation," Brannigan continued, "you'll be willing to read these pages—all these pages."

"I'm willing," I said. "Of course I'm willing. Don't doubt me."

"We didn't mean—"

"I won't be doubted." I sensed my voice rising and, once again, had trouble quelling the sudden rage that gripped me like a tourniquet.

"We won't doubt you."

"We certainly won't."

"Because I understand your church, I know it," I said. "I'm familiar with it. I dated someone from CotM a while back."

Both Brannigan and Raybury broke out with knowing smiles. Brannigan asked for that former girlfriend's name.

"Maddy. Madeline Donaldson."

Recognition passed over the missionaries' faces. Raybury looked to his older companion to take the lead.

"We know her," said Brannigan.

"You do?"

"She's...not very active."

"No," I said. "Not anymore. She may never have truly been."

"No," Raybury said. "She was. Don't doubt us." Then he winked at me.

"We were together almost twenty years ago," I said, "and you know her?"

"Not personally," Brannigan said. "But we know her. We know the names of every one of the Manifested—even those who've tried to leave."

"You can't leave." Raybury's tone was somber, but it perked up with his next words: "Why would you want to? Our Invincible Father is open and understanding of our needs, the girls' as well as the guys'."

"He answers all our prayers," Brannigan affirmed.

Their words I found comforting. To be known. To speak to someone who would understand my needs and desires. Our Invincible Father. Mighty Father. Better than God, or any other god. Stronger.

I showed Brannigan and Raybury the card I'd found on a table at Scotty's. On the front of this church calling card was a picture of an attractive young woman in the arms of her equally attractive—in her eyes—boyfriend, their faces smiling in the glow of the sun rising on the beach in the background. The woman wore an engagement ring. On the back of the card was Brannigan's name and phone number, and above this information the statement *Life CAN be perfect.*

"I want a lot," I said, "and I don't understand why I can't have it."

"Seems like you have a lot already," Raybury ventured.

"I'm hoping you'll understand," I said, my voice again on edge, my volume again inching upward.

"We already understand," said Brannigan. "Go on."

"I want a lot, and at every turn it's looking now like I can't have it. When I was young..."

"What about when you were young."

"When I was young things were different. People weren't so sensitive. They just *were*, you know? We existed. Guys did their thing, girls did theirs. Those were the roles. We played them."

"And now those roles aren't the same," surmised Brannigan.

"I just wish..." I lamented. "I just wish I could feel free again, as a guy."

"As a guy, huh."

"You think I'm whining, don't you."

"Not at all, Stan. Far from it. We hear you," Brannigan said.

"You do."

"We see the changes taking place between guys and girls, that sensitivity as you call it, the touchiness—we see that as a challenge. We're willing to meet that challenge, and we know you'll be willing, too."

"My girlfriend—or, excuse me, *partner*," I spat. "Simone is just as headstrong as I am, and I wish she wasn't. I wish she was just a little more..."

"Submissive," Raybury said.

"You understand."

"Of course we do. We know what it's like out there. And the TV, the social media, what's on the screen, that can only help so much. That's where we step in, Stan."

"My age," I said. "Thirty-six and not married yet, and she lets me know it, she's younger, you know. My habits. My... desires, I guess. My family, or, really, what used to be my family. My—my brother."

The missionaries—together, united—watched me, expectant.

"Did you hear about this?" I showed Brannigan and Raybury my phone.

"CNN?"

"What CNN just reported. The Supreme Court decision. Gay marriage is now the law of the land."

"We did hear," Brannigan said. "It's not a surprise to us. But it bothers you."

"It doesn't bother you?"

Brannigan glanced at the younger missionary before speaking. He seemed to sidestep his own words. "Personally," he said, "it does bother me."

"Me too," piped up Raybury.

"But..."

"But the Church of the Manifested has changed. We're more accommodating than we were, say, twenty years ago."

"The Leader knows it's 2015," Raybury said.

"That's what I thought," I said. "But for me it's personal. My twin brother—my identical twin brother, Jeremy. He's gay."

The 'oh' from both missionaries was barely audible. They shifted on the couch. Their eyes skipped from me to the water glasses before them.

"And I'm not," I said. "I know that about myself. I do. But he.... He used to look just like me. Now he's transitioning, I think it's called."

Brannigan looked up. "He's..."

"I mean he's going through the process of becoming a woman. He says he's wanted to be a woman for so long. He claims that's his true self."

"He's trans?"

"Yes," I said. "He. She. They. How does your church feel about that?"

Raybury exhaled. "That's a whole different..."

Brannigan cleared his throat. His eyes locked with mine. "Of course you want to help your brother, Stan. Am I right?"

I nodded. We remained in our eye-lock.

"We won't turn our backs on your brother. You must know we won't cast him out, or her out, or them out. Whatever they say they are. Not The Church, the only true church. Everyone has a chance to be redeemed through CotM. Everyone has a chance to become Manifested. Have you talked to your brother about this? About not going through with this decision?"

I explained there had never been much point in trying to persuade Jeremy to go back on his decision. He had always, since we were kids, been just as stubborn, just as strong, if not more, than me.

"I believe it is possible to persuade him," Brannigan stated. "Is he here in L.A. now?"

"No. Austin. Texas. With his boyfriend, his partner, Eric. They were waiting for the Supreme Court decision, and now they're going to get married." I laughed. "He's going to get married before me. Wearing a wedding dress."

For a moment, no one spoke. Then Brannigan said, "It may be too late for Jeremy in this life, but in the next..."

"See," Raybury said, "everyone—and I mean everyone, really—joins the Manifested someday, even if they're, you know, dead."

Again I, the enabled, nodded. I felt foolish, powerful.

"I want to understand that about your church—"

"*The* Church."

"*The* Church. The beliefs. The afterlife. What's promised. I only ever went to one service, and it was so long ago."

"You'll go again," Raybury said. "We'll set up a day. Our outpost is in Torrance."

"It's noble you want to help your brother, Stan," said Brannigan. "I can already see you're a good man."

I smiled. "If—"

My phone broke in. All three of us stared at it buzzing on the edge of the coffee table. Brannigan asked if I should pick up. I told him no, this was more important.

"More important than Simone?" Brannigan said. Then, as sheepishly as was possible for him: "I saw the name."

"She can wait," I said.

"A good sign," said Raybury. "A woman who knows to wait."

The first time I spoke to Simone, soon after she was hired as my company's newest receptionist, I could not help but change her last name to that of my own. Paulsen to Pangborn. I pictured the two of us married with kids, a home, two vehicles (one a truck), and my wife home and nurturing. What she was meant for. Simone Pangborn. By all expectations it would work. It had to work. And if it didn't, I wasn't sure what lay in wait.

"She's twelve years younger than me."

"Twelve years?" Raybury whistled.

"Twenty-four," I said. "Lucky me, right?"

"We're glad to hear you're finally planning to marry, Stan," Brannigan said. "Marriage is very important to Invincible Father's plan. We'll get to that plan in future talks. Right now we want to talk to you about the Invincible Spirit. Before we do that, would you allow us to say a prayer?"

I acquiesced and the missionaries bowed their heads.

Instead of clasping their hands, they brought their fists together.

His eyes closed, his forehead pressed against his fists, Brannigan prayed. "Invincible Father. Mighty Father. Thank You for being with us here in Stan Pangborn's apartment in Hermosa Beach. Thank You for allowing him to find our calling card on the restaurant table. It hasn't been easy being here, there's a lot to look at on the beach, many temptations, flesh exposed. We want to thank You for bringing him to us, and we pray that You will give him an understanding of The Church and its teachings so that he may know what we believe is good and true, and he will no longer doubt or fear or show any weakness whatsoever.

"We also pray for You to deliver his brother, his twin, Jeremy Pangborn, who has chosen an unfortunate path. May You bless Jeremy and bring him to us so that he will emerge whole and correct his mistake, accept You and have the chance to join his family in the afterlife."

Both missionaries said *hooyah*. They opened their eyes, and Raybury flipped through his large black Book of the Manifested while Brannigan handed me his own thick copy. He told me to open to a certain page. Already they were preparing me well.

For the rest of that first session, we discussed the Invincible Spirit: how the Invincible Spirit always answers the prayers of all true men who are sincere and unwavering in their faith. Prayers always answered. Some prayers, according to CotM doctrine, take time to answer; Invincible Father might not get to them right away. In some cases, a prayer may take years and years, even decades, to be answered, and if any prayer is not answered in this life, it will certainly be answered in the next.

"That's a big part of what it means to be Manifested," Brannigan said.

"Invincible Father wants to talk to you, Stan," said Raybury. "He wants to talk to all of us, even your brother."

"My soon-to-be sister," I corrected.

While Brannigan and Raybury spoke, I could feel Anxiety's wings lifting on air, my plan congealing like blood on a boulder. No longer did I feel as wicked as I had when they arrived. When they asked if I at all felt Invincible Father's presence in the room now that I'd read a couple passages from the Book of the Manifested, I answered without hesitation, for once believing my own words. "I feel something," I said. "I don't know what, but I feel relieved. It's strange, but I don't feel tense. I'm relaxed right now."

"That's Mighty Father," Raybury said. "That's the Invincible Spirit."

My phone buzzed again as we were finishing up. I did not recognize the number, though the area code was familiar: Austin. Not my brother's—my sister's—number.

I sensed the missionaries watching me. They seemed not to acknowledge the phone but rather focus on me. Waiting for me to speak? On the fourth buzz, I picked up. Though I'd last heard the voice on the other end a decade and a half earlier, it was instantly recognizable.

"Stan."

"Maddy? What—"

"Why I'm calling you? How did I get your number? Jeremy. Stan, I have to talk to you. It's important."

"Uh..." I saw Brannigan and Raybury start to rise. "No,

no," I snapped at them, my finger pressed to the bottom of my phone. "Stay." Then I said to Maddy, "Now's not the best time, but a little later today, yeah. Is that okay?"

"That's fine. Don't blow me off."

"I won't. You'll never believe who I'm with right now."

"A girlfriend?"

"No..."

"Who, Stan?"

"I'll tell you when I call you back, how about that."

"Whatever..."

After the call ended, I said to Brannigan and Raybury, "That was Maddy."

"Madeline Donaldson?"

"We haven't spoken to each other in fifteen years."

Raybury asked why I'd decided to call Maddy in the middle of our talk.

"I didn't call her. She called me."

Brannigan and Raybury looked at each other.

"You picked up the phone, Stan—"

"Because it was ringing."

"—and made the call." Brannigan turned to Raybury. "Right?"

"That's what I saw."

"Whatever you saw is wrong," I said. "The phone buzzed. I picked up. That's all there is to it. I know what she's going to tell me later today."

"What's that?"

"My brother. And, yeah, her brother."

"Were they...?" Brannigan suggested.

"They *are*," I said. "Her brother is my brother's boyfriend. My sister's boyfriend now. And her family's Manifested. So. I'd rather not talk about this anymore. Could we call it a day?"

Brannigan asked when we could meet for the second of the seven Manly Talks, and I said the sooner the better. Brannigan turned to Wednesday, the first of July, and found an open slot—in between the baptism of an elderly man who'd recently lost his wife and the calling on of a family that was struggling with two rebellious teenage daughters.

I smiled as I watched Brannigan pen my name into the light blue chart. Having finished marking me down, the missionary mentioned an Invincible Meeting on Sunday. The Torrance outpost was close. How about visiting?

"That'd be great." I recalled my visit to the Anomar CotM outpost all those years ago with Madeline Donaldson, Maddy-Manifested. I remained shaken by her sudden reinstatement in my life. Shaken and excited and stirred.

"So you and Maddy grew up together?" Raybury asked.

"In Anomar. It's this little town in North San Diego County. Rural."

"Sounds nice," Brannigan said. "And you spoke with the missionaries then?"

"I didn't think about converting then. I was young and... my brother was, well, still my brother. He hadn't come out yet. I only wanted to be with her."

"I hope you're not doing this for Madeline now."

"I'm doing it for Simone," I said. "And myself. And my brother. My father. My future family."

"Good," said Brannigan. "We know there are guys and girls out there who convert just so they can be with their significant other. They might really like someone in The Church just to be with them physically, not spiritually.

Without really believing any of the Mighty Tenets. If that's the case, don't bother. That's not the way to go. I'm here to tell you I don't just believe it, Stan. It goes beyond belief in everything I've been taught. I know. I know the Book of the Manifested is true and that our founder, Conrad Tolson, CT, was a prophet, and The Leader now is a prophet on the level of Our Invincible Father. All men can become gods someday. It is true. So: read and pray. Remember to make the fists, always the fists. Your faith must be sincere. At this point, that's all we ask of you."

He and Raybury took turns shaking my hand, their grips tight as nooses.

And I thought that day, the first of my new life: the Missionaries of the Manifested may be the last true door-to-door salesmen. They represent a part of America's past and a promise of its future.

Two

The beach was an open hand. Maddy and I perched on the concrete wall that separated the pedestrian walkway from the sand before us. Beyond all those sizzling bodies we could see the ocean stocked with boogey- and body-boarders tossed about on the waves. From a distance could be heard the song of that cusp of summer, "Semi-Charmed Life" by Third Eye Blind. I had heard it everywhere this month, our last ever at Anomar High.

I snuck a glance at Maddy, who continued to look ahead and say nothing. Her face was round, her lips heavy, her eyes squinting in the harsh daylight. I wished she would take her clothes off. In the pummeling heat, I wore a shirt, swim trunks and sandals, while Maddy hadn't even tried: she looked as if she were on her way to an anti-war protest. I couldn't understand how she tolerated wearing those dark jeans, the heavy boots, that olive green jacket with the buttons pinned to the lapels. Where was the war? Something in Oklahoma City a couple years ago—but that had been an anomaly, a one-off freakish attack. Maybe something in the Middle East? Or

Africa? Something, somewhere, but not here on Mission Beach. I couldn't understand how she faced the light without sunglasses. I couldn't understand *her*, and it was this lack of understanding that kept me attached to her like a vestigial appendage that should have been severed months earlier. From my perch, I saw some of my classmates, fellow AHS seniors frolicking in the sand, throwing Frisbees, flirting. And did I think to flirt? Did I think to step away from Maddy for even a moment and try talking to another girl, any of whom would be in a bikini and who might have shown some interest in me? It wasn't as if I was unattractive—far from it. It was that I could not understand *her*, and for that reason I could not let her go.

It's because Maddy's Manifested, I thought. But she wouldn't always be, I believed then. She was fighting her religion just as I had fought mine, Catholicism. She was on the outs with CotM. Months earlier she had taken me to the outpost in Anomar and there I had witnessed her engage in a tense debate with a Sunday school teacher who claimed vegetarianism was contrary to the Book of the Manifested's teachings.

She was what The Church called an Out. It was my mission to help her pull free of her religion just as I had broken away from mine a few years before. We would move out of Anomar and attend college together. We would travel, adventure, adult. We would share the same bed and do the things we were meant to do free from any religion.

I wished she would take her clothes off.

I admired her for having the courage at only seventeen to fight against religious oppression. And when she'd been nasty to me lately, it must have been because she was battling her beliefs, her upbringing, her very being—and so couldn't help but disparage me. Stan Non-Man, she called me. Non-Manifested.

Stan Non-Man.

Someday soon, I believed, she would return to how she'd acted toward me in the beginning, when we were good friends and flirting heavily, spending afternoons and evenings together alone, without the parade of Church-affiliated chaperones that was to follow. Someday soon she would shrug off this Church-induced manipulation and get close to me as she did that day when we almost—(alone in my parents' house, Jeremy gone, not there to mess me up, I knew the truth about him even then). Together, Madeline Donaldson and I could return to that time—but in the present. I would rescue her.

Her clothes off.

I asked if she was going to swim. After a time, she answered with the expected "No."

It was and was not my turn to speak. As much as I knew not to give off the impression of eagerness, of insecurity, I so often ended up speaking to her when I shouldn't have, when I should instead have sat back in cool observance and let the silence play out.

—Beat her, Stan. To the quick. Beat her now.

"You're not wearing a swimsuit under that?"

"I don't have a swimsuit," she shot.

You must, I thought, after I'd turned away. I remembered the swim team photo from the most recent AHS yearbook. In that photo Maddy sat on the left edge of the bottom row, her legs drawn up, her knees covering her chest. Her look was accusatory and undeniably sexy. A one-piece.

"Even if I had one I wouldn't go out there."

"Why not?"

"And burn my body? It's stupid. All those people frying themselves like they're meat. It's disgusting."

—I am the silence that is incomprehensible—

Not now. Please.

—and the idea whose remembrance is frequent.

I'm trying to remember this, Jer. I'm trying to remember this *right*.

—Wrong.

"You know Eric called," Maddy said.

—Him.

"Oh. What'd he say?"

"He was upset.'"

"Okay." I didn't know what to do with this information. Maddy looked confused.

She didn't understand I was trying to help, I was her salvation, in a way. We could make a statement against The Church by enjoying ourselves, she showing her skin. If Maddy hadn't bothered to wear a swimsuit, even a one-piece, to Mission Beach for our school-sanctioned Senior Ditch Day, why was she even here? Wasn't she an Out?

—I would be the same soon, brother.

Cute. Real cute. Not the same thing, Jer.

Madeline was staring at me as if I'd grown a third eye.

"What?"

"I wish you'd say something about all this. I wish you'd *care*," she said.

—Good one, brother.

"I'm going swimming," I announced.

Then go in, I anticipated.

"Where's Jeremy?" I thought I heard Maddy say.

I slid off the wall and planted my feet in the scalding sand. "I don't know," I said, though I did.

For a moment our eyes met; each of us knew what the other was thinking. Our brothers together, not this day but last week, the week before last, the coming week, month, year, the far-flung future. Maddy and I knew.

Her parents suspected. Her father made it known in his own quiet way that his eldest son could enter the house if the patriarch was absent. Mrs. Donaldson hoped Eric would get better. He was her boy, climbing the tree on the side of their house as a child, Eric hoisting Maddy up, her shoe resting snugly in the palm of his hand. Brother and sister in her room decorating a handmade birthday card for Dad. Pictures of Mr. Donaldson as a younger man, full-bearded and rugged with Baby Eric on a sling strapped to his back, the two of them ready for adventure. Eric, Maddy's brother. How could he no longer be a part of her family for what he knew and felt to be natural and true? His sister's greatest fear must have been that her brother would not join her in the next life, the Invincible Life. How could he not. He simply could not.

—You who tell the truth about me, lie about me, and you who have lied about me, tell the truth about me.

I left Maddy on the wall and headed toward the water. At the breakers I turned right and followed the shoreline. I took off my shirt. As I walked I stole glances at the women who tanned themselves or played games. I could try for them, couldn't I? Try for someone new.

But not before I understood Maddy.

Up ahead a volleyball game was in progress, and I knew without searching the crowd that my brother was a part of it. Then I saw him: Jeremy, lean and beautiful and flush from the incessant sun. A month away from eighteen, the two of us that day. He was just going up to spike the ball, blocked by Palmer, an equally tall senior. Jeremy sputtered in the sand and his friends, a few of them AHS senior girls, gathered around to help him up. I wanted to laugh with them.

"Stan. What are you doing? Get over here."

"I know," I muttered. I looked around as if there was something better I should be doing at that moment. The other teens on the court beckoned me to join in the fun with shouts of "The Pangborn Twins! Put 'em on different teams! Let 'em go head to head!"

I begged off. "I can't.... Sorry. Gotta swim." With that, I turned and strode to the water. I heard Jeremy call for a sub. He caught up, placed his hand on my shoulder. I lurched forward, and my brother's hand fell away.

He threw his hands up. "Okay.... You don't want to talk..."

I turned to face him. "I want to talk."

A wave crashed into us. I stood my ground, the water past my knees, and dug my toes under the sand. Mole crabs tickled my soles.

"Is it because of Maddy?"

"And more."

Jeremy nodded. Could he come out right then, on Mission Beach, his friends not far away? A little later. Only a little, though: the lie, his life, could not sustain itself.

—Why, you who hate me, do you love me, and hate those who love me?

I know you too well, Jer. Come out with it already. I know you weren't really into Vanessa or Cassie, forced dates. Why—

—Because they wanted to be with me, Stan. Imagine that,

huh. It helped that we were twins. Helped that we were equally handsome. But how shy! The question of our masculinity. The body I never felt comfortable in. On the dance floor at homecoming I pressed my body against Vanessa's, Cassie's at prom, and I thought, What if I were a girl? It took me so long to act on it. Far too long. But I knew then, at a time when I couldn't act on anything. I was starting to fully realize myself, and if I did not appreciate Jeremy Franklin Pangborn, then I couldn't be a partner to anyone. Instead, I flaunted. Flaunted my acerbic sense of humor, all the while fearing the consummation you feared as well. The ultimate act, right? I built up a defense that said Stay away, look but don't touch. Don't involve yourself with me in that way. I wanted to prove to them all they could not possess me. My body belonged to me alone. At night I would have these dreams of lying next to a body, some living body, the two of us naked in bed. A candle flickers from a corner in the room. Shadows thrown. I run my fingers along their back until I find a scar I know will be there, for I created it, then I thrust my fingers through the scar and tear open a fresh wound, seeking out their heart.

Acid trip, Jer? You're on something, no question about that. At least I have a dream that makes sense.

—So, what is it?

I'm at the cusp of the breakers. In the distance, along the zig-zag line I'm treading, two children, a boy and a girl, brother and sister, are sculpting a fortress with their hands. I move toward them, realizing as I walk that I'm not on any beach I know of, and yet it must be San Diego, Torrey Pines or the Coronado strand. The sky is mixed concrete and the wind is harsh, but despite the weather the sand is scorching. As I pass by the brother and sister, the boy says to the girl, *My feet feel like they're being whipped by Pontius Pilate.*

I look down. Footprints before me, larger than my own.

Soon, a man approaches. Not just a man: a transient, and here I am again in familiar territory. He's barefoot, dressed in dark torn jeans and an olive T-shirt, the shirt covered by a nappy flannel windbreaker. His hair is long and tangled and he hasn't shaved in months. It's impossible to understand his eyes. He asks for something—a favor. Exactly what this favor is I can't make out, and suddenly I've rebuked him, and as I'm walking inland, away from the waves, I look over my shoulder and see the bum take a seat in the sand and begin to masturbate, rapidly working his fist, fierce competition. The children are gone. In front of me now is a sliding glass door leading to a stagnant seaside apartment, one of those musty leftover relics in which the décor smacks of the sixties, go-go boots and Vietnam. The room is painted pale sea blue, the curtains lie still. For a moment I stand in the apartment's living room and then, sensing the sliding glass door, I turn, helpless, to watch the homeless man enter the apartment grinning, about to lunge.

—I know what that dream means, Stan. You do too. Your fear—

I have no fear.

—You most certainly do, brother. Fear of intimacy. Of touch. Of contact. Of closeness. Of s—

Don't say it.

—Just three letters? S-E-X?

I'm not afraid of that. I can do it just fine.

—Is that why you're sticking to Madeline Donaldson and her scary church? Is that why you've been so cruel to me?

Aloud, to Jeremy's face, I said, "But I, I am compassionate and I am cruel. Be on your guard!"

My brother laughed. "What was that Dad said when we were kids? He singled you out: 'Don't be so dramatic.'"

"He never said that, not to me."

—On the day when I am close to you, you are far away from me, and on the day when I am far away from you, I am close to you.

That early June day of 1997 on Mission Beach my brother and I nearly came to blows. Cain versus Abel. My money was on Cain.

My brother wheeled around and struck through the waves toward shore. I refused to call out after him. I chose instead to submerge myself. Here, in the cold and dark, my proto-baptism, I could not see or feel or hear my brother. Only my own mind, the thunder, a perfect mind.

"WHAT'S WRONG?"

Brazenly tanned from a slow steady procession of days spent baking her toned body, Simone Paulsen stared through strands of long blond hair that fell around her face. She was more than ready. I reached over from where I sat next to her on my bed and ran my hand down the length of her body. I stroked her thighs, her calves, her ankles, the bottoms of her feet. She sighed, turned her head so that only hair could be seen, and waited.

"Nothing," I said. "You look incredible."

"Then why don't you fuck me."

Taken aback by her bluntness, I kept quiet.

"You can't still be hung up on the f-word, Stan. I told you. I'm not going to say 'make love.' It's so unsexy."

"It's not the f-word."

"Then what is it? Do I really need to be tied up again for you to do it?"

"I told you," I said. "It's my thing."

"And you should know this about me now: my thing is *not* to be tied up or handcuffed every time I have sex with my boyfriend."

"Come on, Sims. You've liked it every time."

"You'd think that. You're in control. All. The. Time."

"So you were lying every time."

"It was hot the first few times, I'll give you that. But now... I want you without being restrained. I mean, Jesus, you want me bound up through the whole thing. I want a little freedom here, Stan."

"I'm tired," I said and felt for what I hoped would be an erection. Nothing there.

"Well I'm tired of doing it the same way every time. We can do this a normal way, okay?"

"Plenty of couples engage in bondage, Sims."

"But every single time? There's something not right about that, Stan."

—She's right, you know.

I slid my boxers off and rolled on top of her. Simone remained on her stomach. I still wasn't erect, but I didn't care. Our bodies fit well together.

"Okay," I whispered.

"Great," she whispered. "Just not there, okay?"

"Why not?"

"Because *it doesn't feel good*, that's why. And plus you're not wearing a condom."

"No condoms."

"Yes condoms." She raised her head slightly. I was finally hard.

"You're on the pill, so—"

"Stan, about th—"

"You feel this, Simone? You feel how hard I am right now, like I should be?"

"That doesn't mean I don't want you to wear a condom."

"Are you shitting me?"

"I'd just feel better about it, okay? Jesus, Stan. Do you have to kill the mood this badly already?"

"How about not tonight," I said. "How about we do it like this. Just like this." I started to move into her.

"No Stan. Stop."

And when I didn't, Simone turned swiftly to the side, throwing me off her. She sat up and stared at me as if I were a rapist.

"What's wrong with you?" she said.

"Nothing's wrong with me. What's wrong with you? You're supposed to be into this stuff."

"Oh am I? Why's that, Stanley?"

"I told you I don't like that."

"I'm not calling you Satan, am I?"

—Those kids at Gordon Lawrence Elementary, brother. Remember all those years of 'if you had an *a* after the *s* in your name you'd be *Satan*!'

"I'm not calling you Simon either."

"Why would I be into everything you've wanted me to do, Stan?"

"Why? Look at you.... You're, you know, beautiful and young and..."

"Oh so the young hot girls are the ones that are always up for *anything*. Is that what you believe in that manosphere of yours?"

"My what?"

"I know you write that blog. *From Adam*."

"You—how?"

"I saw the start of your latest post on your laptop the other day. Jesus, Stan, that's some incredibly reprehensible garbage. You honestly believe all that misogynistic shit you write?"

"No," I said. "I...It's just a persona. Adam. I'm making money off that blog, Simone."

"You make plenty of money at your job, Stan. So you're seriously telling me that everything you're writing about women, about what you think men should do to them, is a lie?"

"Yes!"

Simone was gathering her clothes now. "I would believe you," she said, her eyes still on me, "if I didn't know what you're into in bed."

"That's—that's normal. It's natural."

"It scares me, Stan."

Simone shrank back at my laugh. "*You're* not normal," I said. "*You're* the one who won't let me do what works, what's always worked."

"It worked fine in the pool, Stan. Remember, at my parents' house two weekends ago?"

"I did not enjoy that."

"But *I did*. It was the best sex I've had with you. I finally felt like your equal."

That day at her parents' place in Thousand Oaks, Simone was more than my equal; she was my superior. That afternoon she'd led me from her childhood bedroom into the backyard pool. I was naked by the time she had me up to my neck in water, and I followed her to the ledge that she then perched on, herself naked, and, from her higher vantage point of power, held me as one would a child as I entered her. It felt wrong, our position, the fact that she was the one to hold me, cradle me, my head encircled by her arms, she kissing the top of my head as I thrust.

"You're getting more confident," she'd told me, after we'd finished.

I hadn't felt confident. I wanted to go back to the ropes, the handcuffs, the chains. I wanted all the control. I told Simone as much at that time:

"I...don't like losing control, Simsy," I'd admitted.

"You have to lose control for sex to work, Stan," she'd responded.

"I have to be in control for sex to work for *me*," I said. "Absolute control."

"What about love?"

"What about it."

"Stan. You have to lose control with someone to love them."

Now, in my bedroom in Hermosa Beach, Simone Paulsen dressed herself quickly then stood facing me with her arms crossed. "But you obviously don't want me to be your equal. Christ. All that sick shit you write—"

"It's a *joke*."

"Everything you write is a joke, is that it? Same with everything you say? So you can get *out* of anything you say? Is that how it goes? How you see us? A joke you can get out of?"

"You sound a little unhinged, Sims."

"*I* do? I'm better than this, Stan."

"Sure you are," I said. "But you know there's always somebody better."

"Oh, is that *a threat*?"

"No," I said, backing down. "No. I'm sorry. I'm just...I feel like I'm being attacked...a lot of the time. But I'm getting help now."

"Stan Pangborn? Getting help?"

"Yes. I want to make this work, Simone. I really do. I'm... I'm seeing some people who are going to help me figure us out."

Simone stared at me for several seconds. At last she said, "Are you doing group therapy?"

"In a way, yes. And when the time is right, I'd like to bring you into it, so we can be completely open with each other."

"All right," she said. "Sounds promising."

Hear me in gentleness, and learn of me in roughness.

"Could I, um, could I still fuck you now?"

My girlfriend smiled as she shook her head. "No condom—"

"I'll do it. I promise."

"Do you have any that aren't expired?"

"Ha ha. They're fine. But if I put one on, I'm going to need to..."

"I know."

Simone relented and allowed me to bring out the handcuffs along with the condoms. As she lay back and placed her wrists together, I thought of my former religion, Catholicism.

An old religion, too old. I had once, in the days of Madeline Donaldson, believed religion—any religion—would be absent from the life I shared with my eventual spouse. Religion had always been the problem. My brother's coming out at age eighteen, the summer we graduated high school, was a reaction against religion, a rebellion against the righteous masculinity our father displayed. Jeremy could pull back. He could pull out. He could stay a man. My brother, my twin, myself, could not be gay, could not be queer, could not be trans. In bed, year after year, I would struggle. I would shrink from the body beside me. Why such fear over the act? That vulnerability, that loss of self. What I'd done in Simone's parents' pool—giving her the power, the control over me, the man—was never right. I now saw religion—a certain religion, the one true—as the solution. I would cement my sense of self, my identity. I could not, would not be my brother, my sister. I would live the right way: marry a young woman, Simone, start a family, take my grandchildren to weekly services, get on my knees for the only acceptable reason, keep to my own kind. Jeremy and I had always been different, like the sun above the ocean at night.

Moloch.

THREE

The future president had announced his candidacy for the 2016 election twelve days before the Supreme Court handed down its decision in *Obergefell vs. Hodges*. A decade earlier, in my misguided twenties, I had railed against the president at the time, who'd fashioned himself as a cowboy and sent our country to war. While the war raged, I did too. I kept a blog, *Pangbornapedia*, in which I riffed on current events. I created a series of flyers, each of which depicted a different image of Dubya, underneath which ran the words *George W. Bush speaks American. Shouldn't you?* I posted the series of images and their captions to my blog, put the physical flyers up in well-trafficked spots in Hermosa and Manhattan Beach. My work gained little traction in that nascent social media era—and by 2009 was a shade shy of irrelevant. But then the Tea Party spawned, and I saw an opportunity. A new blog was born. For the past five years, I'd been channeling the frustration-anger-fear of so many willing to roll the dice on anyone but the kind of leader we typically suffer through. The future president would be that unique leader. Like the honey badger, he wouldn't give a shit. Eventually, the majority of the country wouldn't either.

As I watched the future president descend the escalator with his supermodel wife, I knew I would vote for him. He wouldn't win, I thought then, but at least he was good for business. Not only that but I had written so much in support of him and his principles on *From Adam* it made no sense to vote for the woman. She may have had the experience, but she sure didn't have the looks. As I watched I focused on the future president's wife. A goddess, only nine years older than me, it was for her especially I would vote. For the future president's daughter, two years my junior, I would vote. Any man who could convince a woman like that to marry him, and who could produce a daughter as gorgeous as the one he had, deserved any man's support. His money was impressive, but his women were more so. If he were to win, it would be because of his women. It didn't matter if he could lead a country; the whole point was for the country *not* to be led. Volatility. Disorder. Entertainment. These I yearned for at this point in my life, unfulfilled and on the cusp of 36. What mattered to me was that I was certain my brother was voting for the woman. I would vote against Jeremy. I would vote for the underdog. I had always been the underdog.

I turned my attention from the TV to the day's mail. Hardly anything but junk ever appeared anymore. This time, though, a surprise: a postcard from Frank. Greetings from Bulgaria! A collage of stunning beaches, Byzantine ruins, and the elderly cloaked in black astride donkeys. On the back of the postcard, my father had scrawled *Having a great time here by the Black Sea. Simply breathtaking. On our way to Istanbul tomorrow. Hope you're happy with your girl, whoever she is.*

P.S. Hope she's a looker. And a keeper.

I took the postcard to my room and pinned it to the wall above my bed, next to the other postcards my father had sent me during his year-long world tour. Postcards from Europe, Asia, Australia. Postcards from places in the States I had never heard of and would likely never visit. I ached to receive those postcards. I lived through them, I lived through *him*. I would continue to put up each new postcard, provided Frank thought of me, now his only son, in hopes that the man's man who refused to call America 'the States' would return and we could talk face-to-face. In several postcards, Frank wrote of the woman he was with, his Victoria's Secret model of a traveling companion. I wanted to meet this mystery woman.

My phone took ages to reach my ears.

"Madeline."

"Stan. I really didn't think you'd call."

"I felt I should. Our brothers, you know."

"That's what I want to talk to you about. The wedding."

I bit my lower lip, careful not to draw blood this time. "So you know where it'll be, and when it'll be."

"Yes. Austin, now that it's legal."

"And the date?"

"Sunday, August 16th. Eleven in the morning. They thought a Sunday would be appropriate."

"A summer wedding," I said. "In Texas, at the dog-end of summer. What were they thinking?"

"What plenty of other couples are thinking who get married in Texas at the 'dog-end' of summer," Maddy admonished.

"I don't like it."

"So don't go," she said. "I'm only calling you because I

have to. That's my role in this: calling everyone. When I saw you on the list I wondered what Eric and Jeri were thinking—"

"Wait. 'Jerry'? As in 'Ben & Jerry'?"

"No, Stan. J-E-R-I. It's short for *Jeralda*."

"You're shitting me."

Maddy sounded like a kettle releasing steam. "*Think* about showing up, if you even have the decency to do that," she said.

"I'll *think* about it."

"Wonderful. You think about it, Stan. But while you 'think about it,' think about this: showing up to your brother's and my brother's wedding would be a sign you're actually a human being."

"*I'm* the human being," I said. "There's nothing inhuman about *me*. It's you—I never really knew you, Maddy, and you know what? You never really knew me. You don't know what it's like—"

"To have a brother who identifies as queer? I do, Stan."

"No. I mean, the biology...the genetics..."

"Unbelievable, Stanley! You think you're going to 'turn gay' because your brother is?"

"He's my identical twin brother, Maddy. Have a heart."

"*You* have a heart, Stan. But more than that, have common sense. You're so fucking illogical about this. You've been this way forever."

"It's not illogical, Maddy. Research shows—"

"Fuck the research!" she screamed. "You beat the odds, Stan. You're straight. You're a cis male! We all know that. I know that. Congratulations."

My silence seethed. Maddy, not one to ever capitulate,

said, "There. I called you. My job is done here, Stan the Non-Man."

"Didn't think I'd hear that again."

"I had to."

"You didn't have to," I said. "It makes it sound like I'm not..."

"A *man*? Oh, you're *male* all right, Stan. You know what I mean when I say 'Stan Non-Man.'"

"I'm seeing them, Maddy. The missionaries. Two of them, from CotM."

After a moment, Maddy said, "I'm really not surprised. I *thought* you'd go there."

"If I convert I won't ever hear 'Stan the Non-Man' again."

"Dumb reason to convert."

"We could even be together, Madeline."

"I'm married."

My silence spoke for me.

"And you're not, I bet."

"Don't say it like that. I'm seeing someone."

"Another *hot chick*?"

"She's younger," I blurted out, "by a lot. We're really happy together. We're going to get married soon."

"So she's someone you've dated for more than two months this time?"

"Longer than that." (A little longer: close to five months.)

"I don't care to know any more," Maddy said. "There has to be some privacy left in the world."

I was confronted then with a window through which I witnessed Madeline Donaldson, age five or six, seated at the kitchen table, secure in the Anomar house from which her parents would never move. Her mother is doing the dishes, singing a song brought to California by her people, the Manifested, as the nineteenth century gave way to the twentieth. An old trail song kept in tune on the way to freedom. Maddy's mother is younger now, slimmer, and it's summer and outside Eric is scampering while Mr. Donaldson swings in the hammock, his hands pressed to his stomach as if awaiting a child.

Mrs. Donaldson is telling her daughter, "We are a people too, Madeline. We are united because we have been through so much. We are passing tests even now. Someday you'll understand the history, how difficult it is and has been to live Manifested. Father and I will be waiting, and then you'll understand."

The sun is strong and shining savagely throughout the house. The sound of dish against dish, water running in the sink and under her mother's hands. Having finished, Mrs. Donaldson opens a cupboard, brings out a jar of peanut butter. She opens it, frowns at what she sees inside. "Who put her hands in the peanut butter jar?" she says, her voice that of a little girl, younger than her daughter. It's a toddler's voice. Madeline watches her mother set the jar on the counter and take up a butter knife. Her mother approaches her. Young Madeline balls her hands into fists and lays them on the table. Her mother takes the butter knife by the blade and raps her daughter on the knuckles with the heavy handle while saying *Who put her hands in the peanut butter jar* as many times as it takes before her daughter screams *I did.*

"Goodbye, Stan. If you're at the wedding, I'll be sure to avoid you."

I think I trust him more than I trust myself. Mom knows the end of the world is coming soon because men at church are telling her that. I wonder if she's ever going to accept the fact that I am NEVER going to be Manifested again. I can't have any contact with her because she is obsessed with convincing me that I need to be Manifested. I honestly don't know which is worse: assuming a false identity and being tormented internally or embracing a true identity and being disowned by my family. I have decided to embrace my own identity, but I still cry a lot. How can I not when the people who raised me see me ONLY as someone who does not go to outpost on Sundays? Why does it matter that I am their son and brother? I just don't know how to make myself happy being something I'm not.

    Don't give up.
    Just tell me what you really mean
    Why do you do that
    Would you tell me the truth
    Horrible things you do to me
    That was mean
    I didn't mean to do that
    Neither did I
    I'm sorry
    I scared you off
    I made you uncomfortable
    Finally I feel guilty
    I'm so attracted to you

I set my phone down and stared at it longer than it had taken to speak with Maddy. Remembering my time in Anomar with the Manifested. Madeline Donaldson had been my first kiss, my first foreplay and my first heartbreak. My body had responded shockingly well to hers. She had made me strong, virile, just like one of the Manifested. I would have followed her to college that summer of '97, the summer

Jeremy came out, Frank moved out and my brother and I left for our respective colleges, Stan to L.A. and Jeremy to N.Y., stranding our mother. That summer Maddy had revealed she was seeing someone, a socially confident born-again who'd graduated AHS the previous year. I was incensed at the revelation of her affair. *Affair?* Maddy had scoffed. *What are you talking about?* She claimed she and I hadn't been dating, I had never been her boyfriend—a lie from the moment the words left her lips. We had gotten so terribly close that one day at my house, only for her to tell me she didn't want a relationship with *any* guy, certainly not anything sexual. She, like me, feared sex. Yet there she was writing questions like *Should I have sex with Andy?* in her diary, which I hadn't meant to read but I happened to see lying open that time I was at her house that summer. It didn't matter that I wasn't Manifested, I realized then. It mattered that I wasn't religious. She'd lied, she'd cheated on me, and I'd let the revelation of her affair hold me back for years. After Maddy there had been, what? Nothing in the way of lasting connections. True, I was young and inexperienced at the time, but that was no excuse for why I found it difficult to perform after the move from Anomar and the Manifested. It did not excuse my twin's sexuality.

Do you work in marketing or are you studying it?
    How did you get into marketing?
    What is your background?
    What would be your dream marketing job?
    What sort of products or services do you deal with?
    Which areas of marketing are most interesting to you?
    What does your job involve on a day-to-day basis?

Is your company marketing-oriented?

What is your job title?

What do you have in common with the other members of this group?

I STARED OUT THE WINDOW, astonished at the annihilation underway. Trees had toppled, while others keeled over into rising water. Electrical lines writhed in the rushing current, and cars drifted into each other like bumper boats.

The train shook and heaved as it gyrated. I touched my fingertips to the cold condensation on the window and continued to observe. I was not safe, not really. A tree could crash through the roof of the train car and bash my brains out. The train could derail and I could drown in a foot of water. They could shut down the tracks ahead and I would be forced to subsist on rainwater and what few snacks I'd brought. Anything could happen. I feared like Frank and Linda feared. But whereas the previous fear had been attributed to events brought on by fate or bad luck, the fear now was based on the spiritual power above. Things didn't just happen—I now saw them happening for a reason. The hurricane was an Act of God, sent to New York to punish me for visiting my brother. To punish all people for living in sin. Such a clear sign that it struck here, north of the city.

A large man stood in the aisle and looked out either side at the unfolding calamity. "They closed the tracks down back," he said to another man, his girlfriend or wife or daughter seated close by. "We'll push through to Poughkeep-sie, but this is the last train out today." He clutched a cell phone, still an infrequent sight in that final year of the 1990s.

Exhilarated I had caught the last train out of the city for upstate. I had nearly missed the chance to see Jeremy, and I needed to talk important matters with him in person. Our meeting would not be in vain. We were 20 and needed to be in the same room that night.

Greater than my fear of the storm, of God's fury unleashed, was the fear that my brother would not be there to meet me at the station. From Poughkeepsie to Annandale-on-Hudson was not a short drive, I imagined, and the last we'd talked, Jeremy was still not sure he could scrounge up a ride. What if my brother did not show? How would I fend for myself then?

I hated to think how dependent I was on him now. I had—

—Now? What do you mean *now*, Stan? You've *always* needed me.

I thought when Jeremy said he was going to college in New York he meant Manhattan, NYC, The City, or at least one of the other boroughs. I did not picture a small liberal arts college over a hundred miles north of Gotham.

The underbelly of the train shrieked and clawed.

My fears proved unfounded, for when I walked into the dimly lit station, Jeremy strode in, looked around and, spotting his brother, leaped forward to give him a hug. We exchanged some small warmth and comfort.

"You look—"

"—like I've died and gone to hell. I know. You don't look so good yourself. I caught the last train out."

"I heard. They're not letting anything else up here. This

Floyd is a monster. But you lucked out, bro. Power's completely out across campus, including the apartments."

I groaned.

"None of that now," Jeremy said. "I want you upbeat to the end."

Late that night in Jeremy's room, we lay in darkness listening to the tendrils of hurricane force lash against the building. Neither of us had said anything since finishing off the last of the liquor and saying goodnight to the group gathered in the candlelit common area. Jeremy's friends, all of whom I had judged within seconds of saying hello. Throughout the course of the evening and well into the late hours, I'd remained silent and said few words, the most vocal of which was the 'goodnight' uttered while heading to bed.

"This is God's doing," I said to break the darkness.

"What is."

"This...storm."

"Hurricane Floyd? God's doing? You're talking out your ass, Stan."

"Out *my* ass? That's funny, coming from you."

Alarmed, my brother sat up. A strike of light flashed across his face.

"Stan. Why did you come here?"

"To see you."

"You didn't come here to see me. I don't know what you came here for."

"I need to talk to you."

He mock-laughed. "Is that all? Well, I'm right here, bro. Let's talk."

"Where'd he get that scar?"

"...You mean Ben, my friend?"

"The guy with the guitar. The guy who gave us a ride from the station."

"I don't know, Stan. I've never asked. Does it matter?"

"Of course it matters. It matters that you've been dodging talking about your problem."

A long silence followed. When at last Jeremy answered, his voice was shaky with rage and sorrow. "What would my problem be?"

"Your problem is my problem. I don't blame you. I blame it. *It.*"

Jeremy spoke carefully, his voice a hiss escaping a pressure cooker. "What is my problem?"

"Our problem," I said. "*Our* problem."

"'And then my mother conceived such a great few,'" my brother said, "'she gave birth to twins: fear and I together.' Pretty obvious who's Fear here."

"I know you've felt fear just as much as I have, even more I'm sure, over what you're doing to your—"

With a cry, Jeremy rolled over and fell on top of my sleeping bag beside his bed. He held me down and placed a hand over my mouth. The other hand was on my neck. At first, I did not struggle. I listened.

"What is it?" my brother said. "What makes it so bad? What is so wrong with it? Is it the act itself? It has to be more than just the sight of someone different, doing something different. The sight of us holding hands and kissing. It's sex, it's always been. *The act.* The thought of me opening myself up. Does that make you feel sick or something? Less of a 'man'? Do you really worry about *me*, or is that just an excuse to cover for your worry over yourself?"

"It's about..." I struggled to breathe. "About the country...the way we're going as a people. Families are falling apart. Look at ours!"

My brother eased up on my neck. "That's fucked up thinking, Stan. Dad would've left even if I hadn't come out. Even if I was straight, he still would have left."

"Not true."

"Dad has his own problems, and you know it, even if you won't admit it."

"He's not even your dad anymore."

"That may be true. Be still." He pinned me back down. "It's not like it used to be. Not like I can't overpower you now. What if I decide to have a family? What if I was the 'wife' in my marriage? Would that mean you're a woman? Because we're the same? We're not the same, Stan. We're so different from each other."

"Our family was perfect," I spat out, "before you felt you had to confess."

Jeremy loosened his grip and let his hands fall away completely. He leaned his head back against the bed while I sat up and rubbed my throat.

"Dad—Frank," Jeremy said quietly. "He's not the man you admire. He's not that kind of man..."

"I don't want to hear it."

"Believe what you want to believe, Stan, and I'll believe the truth."

I clasped my hands and closed my eyes. "I am the slave of him who prepared me," I said.

—No question there. You know what, Stan? I am the one who is honored, and who is praised, and who is despised scornfully.

I am peace—

—You're not peace. *I* am peace, and war has come because of me.

Jer...

—And I am an alien and a citizen. You—you, Stan, are the substance and the one who has no substance. An image of you, brother, as a kid: At an edge of the Gordon Lawrence playground, alone, poking ants with a gnarled stick.

"The truth," said Jeremy, "was looking you in the face every day we woke up to Frank Pangborn. You know when he was in college, before he met Mom, he was really close to this guy, and one—"

"Liar!" I yelled. "Whatever happened didn't. He would never tell you something like that."

"He didn't. His mother did. On her deathbed. You remember how I was the only one bothered to visit her."

"She made it up then. Out of spite."

"Sure. Out of spite."

"It's not true," I said. "Not true."

"Didn't take you long to get back on religion," Jeremy said. "I thought the Church of the Manifested and the whole fallout with Madeline would be the end of it. I don't know what you're doing—"

"I'm trying to help you!"

"Come on, Stan. Look at me. Do *I* look like *I* need help? Why don't you turn on the lights and look in the mirror. See what you can see. You need a scapegoat for your failures, and religion helps fit the bill. At AHS it was the Manifested. In college, I don't know what it is, or what it's going to be."

"You're full of it. I don't have any failures."

"Your failure with women—your *fear* of women."

"I don't fear women. You're the one—"

"You fear anyone different from you."

"Jesus, listen to this."

"How about this. How about we talk about *your* problems, Stan. How you have so few relationships—and they all end abruptly. You avoid people, you let friendships fade. You don't understand that people are important too. Have you even once called any of the gang from AHS since we graduated, even once?"

I paid my attention to the battered window and said nothing.

Jeremy's laugh was curt. "Remember," he said, "remember when we went to see *Chasing Amy* our senior year, and you insisted we sit one seat apart from each other?"

"It wasn't just my—"

"Sure, sure. But there we were, six or seven of us guys, all supposedly friends, all seated at least one seat apart in the theater. I think you had two seats between you and me."

"Last time we saw a movie together," I said.

"Last time we did anything together, until now."

The rain struck the window in great sweeping waves. When next Jeremy spoke the rage was gone from his voice, leaving only the sorrow. "You blame Maddy for dumping you? The one or two other girls you've been with? You think my sexuality caused your anxiety with them? That is utter cowshit, man. That's all you, Stan. You're straight. I know you are. Stop thinking I'm the cause of your lack of confidence."

I can't touch you anymore.

"If by perfect family you mean Mom and Frank arguing over money, the house, where Dad was all the time..."

My vagina deserves better than this.

"…Frank's numerous affairs that you think make him an admirable man…"

Are you gay?

"No family is perfect, Stanley. Not one in this world."

What about the next world?

I am control and the uncontrollable.

I am the union and the dissolution.

I am the abiding and I am the dissolution.

I am the judgment and the acquittal.

"I'm sorry," I said suddenly. "I shouldn't be here. I'll go—"

"Wait till dawn," Jeremy said. "The storm may let up by then."

Bereft of strength now, my brother managed to crawl into bed, turn the covers up and twist on his side away from me. I did not wrest my attention from the weeping window.

"Stan."

"What."

"We're three months away from the next decade, the 21st century. You live in L.A., surrounded by so much culture and diversity. And yet…. Time has stopped for you. See that it starts up again soon."

He wished me a good night. I did not do the same.

FOUR

On her prom night, Simone stayed at a fancy hotel with her then-boyfriend Jonathan. On the way up to their room, Jonathan's anger over the way he'd seen Simone look at another guy on the dance floor spiked and he pushed her down the long flight of stairs. Simone hit several steps before she was able to stop herself. Although hurt, she was relieved to not be embarrassed: no one had seen; Jonathan had made sure of that. It was 2009 and everyone had a phone. Someone would have taken footage of her rolling down the staircase in her expensive dress—which meant everyone would have seen.

It couldn't have just been the look she gave; Simone swore what really ticked Jonathan off was the fact she'd insisted on trying on his tuxedo before they headed out for the evening. He relented only when she promised she'd make it worth his while in the hotel room after the dance. Jonathan reluctantly took a picture of the tuxedo-clad Simone. In the photo she is beaming, her eyes bright. "All right, get out of that," Jonathan had said after he'd snapped the picture. He never asked why she'd wanted to dress up in a guy's suit. I wasn't about to ask either.

Even after the hotel assault, Simone stuck with Jonathan. Having a boyfriend mattered to her. She stuck with him even after watching one night as he, high and savagely drunk, brandished a revved-up chainsaw at a backyard mixer in front of his buddies, all of whom were too wasted to care. Simone wanted out, but Jonathan's parents were steadfast friends with her folks, and he felt entitled to her in a way that pre-absolved him of all responsibility and guilt. If she were to leave Jonathan, Simone believed, she would betray her parents and his parents, their families. She stayed far too long, a decision she would regret. In the end, Jonathan dumped her because, in his words, he wanted to sleep with a lot of women.

Simone had told me all this on our second date, and I'd promised I would never be a Jonathan to her. I was a man, but I was not cruel, not an abuser.

"How was that?"

"Fine," Simone said.

I let the last of the chains fall to the sides of her body. My girlfriend of a few months shook her arms and pushed all that metal to the edge of the bed.

"You sure?"

"Yes, Stan. I'm sure."

"Was I..." I could not bring myself to say it.

Simone sighed. "Yes, Stan. You were."

As we both dressed, Simone wouldn't look at me. At last, she said, "Why are you taking tomorrow afternoon off?"

"How'd you find out about that?"

"Theresa told me. You have a doctor's appointment or something?"

I hesitated, on the edge of a lie that refused to live on my tongue.

"No appointment," I said. "Not a medical one anyway."

"So, you do have an appointment."

"I do," I said. "I'm seeing two people. The…"

"The therapists? That's right. You are doing that."

"They're not therapists. They're, um, missionaries."

Now Simone looked at me. Wary. Concerned. Upset.

"Why, Stan?"

"Because it's going to help me. It's helping me already. And it's going to help us."

Simone scoffed before speaking. "No religion can help us," she said.

"This one will. The Church of the Manifested."

The sound Simone expelled at my revelation recalled the cry of a wounded animal. She stepped back, in the direction of the doorway.

"You're seeing Manifested missionaries." She laughed, incredulous.

"So?"

"You told me early on you haven't been to a church in years, and now you're getting involved with the Church of the Manifested. It's not even a religion, Stan."

"It is too!" I said.

"Oh shit," Simone said. She stared. "You're going to convert."

"I didn't say that. Right now we're just talking."

"Conversion talks, Stan."

"They're called Manly Talks, Simone."

"Same thing. I know all about CotM."

"You do?"

"I dated a Manifested guy. And now you're..."

This 'Manifested guy' followed Jonathan. Simone had never mentioned him before. His name was Xavier; Simone had met him at a beach clean-up while in her sophomore year of college. They'd dated for close to three years before Simone finally called it off. That would mean Simone had only dated two long-term boyfriends.

"You're doing this because of me, Stan. Right?"

"I'm doing this because of *me*. I've been just outside the Manifested, looking in, since I was seventeen."

"And now you want in. To get to me. There's no other explanation."

"You don't know me," I said.

"No. I don't," she said. I saw now she stood in the doorway to my room. "And that's the problem," Simone continued. "Are you the Adam online, the one who posts those awful things, creates those awful memes and gets all those likes from, god, who knows what freaks are on there. Is that you, or is that just a front like you say it is?"

After a moment, she added, "I truly believe you hate me, Stan."

"I don't hate you," I said. "I—" I almost said 'I love you' but censored myself in time. It would not have been true. I did not love Simone. But I could. Through the Church of the Manifested, I could.

"This is not love," Simone said. She gestured to the chains on the bed as she spoke. "It can't lead to anything like love."

"Plenty of girls love what I love, Simone. They must."

"Then find those girls, Stan. It's not for me. It's scary. But what's even scarier is this thing you have with CotM. You just assumed I'd be fine with it?"

"I thought we could talk with them together."

"Go through the Manly Talks together? Listen to all the Manifested's misogynistic patriarchal psycho-babble? I already went through all that, Stan. I lived it, and I suffered."

Her words poured out. She told me how enamored she had been with Xavier when they first met. He wasn't as handsome as Jonathan, athletic or outgoing, but the lack of these qualities was exactly what she found attractive. What mattered most was that Xavier was different from her previous boyfriend. He was bookish, quiet, slender. Simone liked that he didn't smile a lot; toward the end of her time with Jonathan, she could no longer trust his smiles. For a while she and Xavier made sense. They did so many great things together, and at one point Simone thought she might be falling in love. It was strange not to have the pressure of sex forced on her. She viewed Xavier as mature, confident, secure.

Wrong. It wasn't that Xavier was immature and unconfident and insecure. He was simply disinterested. Frighteningly disinterested, in fact. Several months passed before he took her bra off, several more before her jeans dropped. No matter what she did, what she said, how she moved, how she dressed, how she lay, how she touched, how she urged him to touch, nothing happened. Nothing—or at most very little. Most nights they would lie side-by-side in bed, more often hers, not touching. Eventually, they would fall asleep without having done so much as given each other a chaste good night kiss. At first, Simone found this strangely exciting. She fantasized about what would happen after the delay; it would certainly put anything she'd done with Jonathan to shame. But the delay never ended. Frustrated, Simone felt she should say something, but she was awful at expressing herself then.

Finally, toward the end of their time together in college, Simone did bring up the subject of sex. Xavier could no longer avoid it. One night, while they were again naked and lying next to one another without touching, he told her the truth. He told her exactly why he held off having sex.

"I'm waiting," he said, "to see if I can completely control you before I commit."

Simone recoiled, and when she expressed confusion, Xavier explained: As a member of CotM who was not yet Max Manifested, he had to search for the perfect girl, or The Perfect, as the Church called this being, and once he found his Perfect, he had to work on her. *Working on her* meant convincing his Perfect to join The Church of the Manifested. Xavier was working on Simone now. The ultimate test of her commitment to him, and to the Church, was his mission. If she could remain faithful to him while he proselytized, they were meant to be together in this life and in the next.

"I don't understand," said Simone after hearing all this, "how withholding sex is 'working on me.'"

Xavier stared her down and smiled. "You're still with me, aren't you?"

Simone figured the Church of the Manifested was to blame. They had brainwashed her boyfriend, who was otherwise innocent. If it hadn't been for CotM's involvement, Xavier would have been just another guy. Instead he did its bidding; she assumed he would face punishment if he did not. He wanted to have sex with Simone, he really did, but The Church weighed on his shoulders and he could not shrug it off. Xavier promised he would reevaluate his position in The Church when he returned from his mission, before his confirmation and Max Manifestation. If, after her boyfriend returned from his year-long mission, Simone no longer felt CotM was worth her commitment, Xavier would break from The Church and return to Simone a new and changed man.

Simone believed him. She was almost 22 at the time and about to graduate from college. She did not know what to do with her life beyond get a job and somehow stay with Xavier, who told her often that he loved her and meant it. His love, though all but absent in the bedroom, was shown in so many other ways that it seemed to her more real, purer and truer than anything Jonathan or any other potential boyfriend could give her. In truth, she did not want to find a new boyfriend, not when she had been with Xavier for so long. They must have been right for each other, and when at last they did sleep together in the way couples are supposed to sleep together, the waiting would prove worthwhile.

Simone waited. After his college graduation, Xavier flew to South Africa and Simone went to work in L.A. She changed jobs a few times, but although she had hopes for Xavier, her boyfriend's attitude and beliefs did not change. Worse, he only seemed more under CotM's power now that he was on his mission. Maybe it was his companion, the fellow missionary who had to be with him at all times so that neither Manifested would be tempted—not even by a passing glance their way. Maybe it was his mother who wrote to him even more than Simone did. Still maybe it was the isolation, the lack of anything not having to do with the Church of the Manifested, the long hours, the living conditions, The Church itself. Simone was convinced her letters were either being censored or outright not being delivered. Did they have the mark of a Non-Manifested on them?

As for Xavier's letters, they turned more bizarre as the

months passed. By the ninth month, Xavier had stopped mentioning Simone entirely. These later letters were addressed to Invincible Father, Mighty Father, Manly Father. They quoted scripture, passages from the Book of the Manifested. They encouraged all faithless men to do good works by obeying The Leader and entering the Manosphere online. They urged all Non-Manifested, especially women, to seek spiritual guidance from the missionaries. To Simone, these were terrifying letters that testified to her boyfriend's loneliness and increasing mental instability. Xavier must have been detached from reality; The Church had made him so.

Many times, Simone thought of flying to South Africa to save her boyfriend simply because he was still her boyfriend and she had no other. But, saddled with thousands of dollars in student loan debt, she hadn't sufficient funds to make the trek, and so she did nothing as Xavier finished off his mission and returned to the U.S. Only he did not return to California. He settled in Flagstaff, Arizona.

"He's there," Simone said, "because the Church of the Manifested's headquarters is in Phoenix. I know. I tried calling his parents.... They were always a little weird with me, but when I called the last time, they told me he was doing fine and was engaged. He had found his Perfect, they said. Happiness just consumed them like a monster, I could hear it in my heart. I swear I could see their smiles. They asked me how I was doing. It was so superficial, I would've cried if I hadn't been so angry. It's like I had put so much into this guy, and for what? I'm never going to understand what happened. I spent years thinking I could change him. That he could change..."

"Some men can't change," I said.

"No man can truly ever change, I think."

"I see how you feel about The Church," I said. "But it won't be the same experience when you and I go through the talks."

Simone looked shocked, which surprised me. I really did try to listen to what she said next: "Seriously, Stan? Are you for real? You just listened to all that, the whole story of my last several years, and all you can say is that it's going to be different when we convert to the religion I despise? God, you're one of them already."

She shook her head and leaned against the door frame. The pity she showed caused my fists to clench.

"Why wouldn't you try this with me? The Church has made changes. It's not the same as it was even a year ago. I promise. You know I'm not Xavier, and I'm certainly not Jonathan."

"I'm getting out of here, Stan. Have fun with your cult."

"It's not a cult!" I rose from the bed and advanced toward her. Simone backed out of the bedroom.

"Stan..."

I pursued her through the hallway, then the living room, only to stop at the front door.

"It does not brainwash people. It's not some devil-worshiping secret sect. It's right is what it is. It's over a hundred years old. It's part of this country now. Everything about it, how it was founded to what it stands for—you can't get more American. It's going to be the next world religion. You'll see."

But those last words were spoken to the door that had moments before closed behind my ex.

. . .

THAT NIGHT, in a blessed vision, I was visited by the future president. He lay on my couch watching TV, and when I approached him, he made room for me.

"Thank you for visiting me, of all people," I said.

"You're not a person," he said. "You're special, Stan."

"I'm so confused. I feel this...rage, all the time. I don't know where it comes from."

"I know where it comes from. I know exactly what it's like. I too am of two minds."

"Two minds? You?"

"Conflicted. I am the one who is disgraced and the great one."

"You are," I said.

"Give heed to me, for I am knowledge and ignorance, I am shame and boldness, I am shameless; I am ashamed."

"You are."

"I am strength and I am fear."

"You are!"

"I am war and peace."

"*You are!*"

"I am the one who has been hated everywhere, and who has been loved everywhere."

On the TV was the future president, seated behind a grand desk. He pointed his finger at the camera and scowled. Uncle Sam I am, I thought.

"Your problem, Stan, is the problem of this country. The division. The divisiveness. The two minds, the two souls. The two sides. The fact that no one can agree, all those arguments and different beliefs. When I'm in charge there won't be any division, there won't be any debate. Sides will cease to exist. Parties will cease to exist. No more politics, no more arguments, no more differences. No more questioning things that don't need to be questioned. No more thinking about things that don't need to be thought about. With me as the leader, everyone will agree, every citizen safe and happy. A country where *everyone* is of the same mind. These states will be united for the first time in their history."

"I can just picture it," I said, my eyes closed. "Just picture it."

"I can fix it, and I will fix it. Watch."

Now the TV showed a grand hotel suite, morning, a bed in which a young man and a young woman slept with the covers thrown over them. Close up on the beautiful blonde's face. The sound of a key inserted into a lock, a door opening. The woman, early 20s, wakes up. She glances at the man next to her and then gasps when she sees another young woman enter the suite. This young woman, also early 20s, dark-haired and severe-looking, wears an Eminem T-shirt and workout shorts. Behind her stands the future president. He's younger, carries less weight, and wears a burgundy bathrobe. The dark-haired woman in front of him looks as if she hasn't slept at all. The sharp-eyed future president looks expectant, pleased.

"What's going on?" the blonde says.

"Son!" the future president barks. "Wake up!"

The blonde shakes the young man. "DJ!" she says. "DJ! Your dad's here. Wake up!"

"Huhn..."

"Wake up!" the blonde says. "What is this? What the fuck is going on? Is he supposed to be here?"

The young man sits up. He is shirtless. "Dad, I..."

The future president orders his son to leave the suite.

"Dad..."

"Get out."

"Oh fuck…" The young man holds his balled fists against his eyes. "Oh fuck oh fuck oh fuck!"

"DJ," the blonde implores. "Talk to me. What is your dad doing in your room?"

"Fuck fuck fuck!"

"DJ!"

The young man can't look at the blonde or the brunette as he gets up and, naked, leaves the room.

The dark-haired young woman hisses a word—*trus*—at the young man as he passes her by.

The door shuts loudly. The blonde sits up but keeps the covers pulled over her chest.

"What the fuck is this?" she again asks. "Is this part of the interview?"

"The interview concluded hours ago, Amber," the future president says. "You have my offer. I trust you'll say yes. But even if you don't…. No matter what you say now, this is still going to happen."

The brunette looks crestfallen, resigned. The future president smiles. "I want you two to get ready. I'm going to get ready too. When I come out, I expect you'll know how to appear."

"Is this real?" I asked the future president seated next to me. "Did this really happen? Is that really you? Is this a documentary?"

"It's just incredible, what they'll do for you. Watch."

On the screen the future president heads to the bathroom. He leaves the door slightly ajar. The sound of running water.

"I'm getting the fuck out of here," the blonde, Amber, says.

"You are an idiot if you do," the brunette announces. A Russian accent.

The brunette drops her workout shorts to reveal her skimpy underwear. She starts to take off her Eminem shirt.

"You don't have to do that," Amber says.

"*Nichego.*"

"What?"

"It's nothing. It does not matter."

Amber points the remote at the TV. "He's been on TV," she says. "Maybe this'll distract him."

The brunette holds on to the bottom of her shirt and does not take it off. She stares at the screen. On it, CNN is showing the World Trade Center. The North Tower is on fire.

"Oh my God—" Amber says. "What the—"

"No. Oh no," the brunette says. "It's today. It's this morning."

"What do you mean?"

The brunette moves toward the TV. "Their plan," she says. "They planned this. DJ, his father, his family…"

"That?!?"

Amber points at the TV. As she does—in the midst of the CNN anchor interviewing an eyewitness by speakerphone—a passenger jet barrels into the South Tower.

"Oh shit! Was that—"

"The other one!" the brunette cries. "They have to destroy both!"

"I don't—"

"Hanif was supposed to be on one of those planes! He refused, he escaped. And they killed him!"

"The terrorists?"

The brunette shakes her head. "He gave the order. For the

murder of Hanif. He's responsible for *all* of that." She indicates the twin towers burning on TV.

"Who?"

The brunette pivots and points. "Him!" she screams. "The Developer!"

Amber looks to where the brunette points accusingly at the future president, who stands a short distance away with his hands in the pockets of his bathrobe. He is expressionless. He orders the brunette to sit down.

"No."

"Get out of the way."

"Fuck you!"

"You're blocking my view!" the enraged future president shouts.

The brunette's laugh is something of a shriek.

"I want to watch this!" the future president says.

"So you can see your plan?" The brunette turns to Amber. "He's going to build something in place of the towers. Something of his own. And make so much money from it, forever and forever."

"No..."

"He's clearing the area. He's making room for his real estate, his proper—"

The brunette's chest bursts with spattering blood, the entry wound in the middle of Eminem's forehead. She stares down at the gaping hole in her shirt. She tries to say something, but instead of words only blood trickles over her lips. She collapses, leaving the TV with its images of the September 11th terrorist attacks on the WTC in full view.

Amber, in shock, stares, her mouth open. Then she screams. Her eyes dart from the TV to the carpet, where the brunette lies dead, and then to the future president, who stands holding a gun. Amber continues screaming. She pulls the covers up around her farther, as if they can hide her away.

"I don't think it's necessary to watch anymore," I said. This experience no longer felt like a vision.

"But this is the best part," the future president said. He slid closer to me and bade me watch.

On screen, the future president says, "Stop right now." Amber, her eyes on the gun, ceases screaming. She composes herself enough to speak. Her voice is ragged. "You fucking shot her," she says.

"I had to," the future president says. "She would have killed you."

Amber, incredulous, laughs. "What? You're out of your mind."

The future president inches toward her as he speaks. "I told you I was your savior, Amber. She was in league with them, Hanif and all of them, she was a terrorist too, trying to turn you against your own country."

"I don't believe it."

"What do you believe?"

"I believe what she said. That you..." Amber trails off. She shakes her head at what's running through her mind. The future president fills it for her:

"That I conspired with terrorists in the Middle East to have them fly a plane each into the World Trade Center towers, allowing me to build my own tower in their place."

Whether through shock or exhaustion or both, Amber laughs. It's a small laugh that grows stronger when the future president joins her. As Amber laughs, tears stream down her cheeks. She uses the covers to dab her eyes. "It's so absurd," she says.

"Far more absurd than the truth."

"What is the truth? Please. What is it?"

A lull. They both watch the TV.

"If you can't prove it didn't happen, then it happened," the future president says. He then tells Amber directly, "You're a clever girl. Expert with the look of things. I need you. DJ needs you. My entire family needs you. Do you believe that?"

"You shot her."

"I can shoot anyone. Anyone can shoot anyone. Do you want to shoot me?

Amber stays silent.

"We all need you, Amber. Do you believe that?"

"Yes. I do."

"Good. That's all you need to believe. Twenty years from now they'll still be floating that this was an inside job, the Little Bush planned it to make sure he wouldn't go down as the most forgettable president ever. That won't happen to me. I won't be forgettable. I need you, Amber. This..." The future president gestures to the TV and the brunette's body beneath it. "This can be fixed. All this can be made right. Our country can be made right again, after today. But I'm going to need your help. I'm going to need your commitment, your sacrifice, your secrecy. And in return..."

"Yes."

"You will never be afraid again."

Amber sobs quietly. The future president sits down beside her and takes her hand in his own. Amber nods and dabs her eyes.

My TV snapped off. In the darkness of my living room, the future president said, "How'd you like the show?"

"Freedom Tower," I said. "It's yours."

"I can fix everything," the future president said. "I will fix everything."

"I know you will," I said. "I can't wait."

Five days after the towers fell, I visited Mother of Mercy in Anomar. A new priest was there, having years earlier replaced Father Melvin.

"I'm here to make a confession."

The priest looked up from his papers. He wore wire frames, and what remained of his hair stuck out of his scalp in wisps.

"Can it wait?"

Together, we left his office and went around the front of the administration building to the adjacent church. White stucco and wooden beams, the Catholic cradle of my childhood would never cease to remind me of the plaster-of-paris missions Frank helped his sons make when they were at Gordon Lawrence Elementary.

All the pews stood empty. On the dais behind the altar, a man rubbed the feet of the crucified Christ. I thought to get down on one knee and make the sign of the cross, but I'd forgotten how to do it—was it right to left or left to right? What was the quick action Frank had done with his thumb against his forehead—or was it his chin, or both? A double tap. Too afraid to risk embarrassment, I kept walking.

The solid window slid to the side, and the priest's face showed through the wire-mesh screen.

"Tell me your sins, my son."

"It's difficult, Father."

"Do your best. It's a challenging time. The country is headed to war. Vengeance is business now. Do you wish to harm those who attacked us?"

"Not really," I said. "But I do want to harm."

"Who?" The priest sounded like an owl. "Who?"

"My brother. Maybe his boyfriend. They're in New York, but they weren't anywhere near the attacks, of course."

The priest coughed uncomfortably. His Adam's apple disappeared. His next words came out in a croak. "Why do them harm?"

"They're a weakness in our country, Father. They weakened us enough to allow the terrorists to attack."

The priest tried to laugh off what he'd just heard. "That makes no sense."

His smile fell to fear when he saw my look. It was the look, he would later say to his colleagues but to no one else, of wickedness. If the devil had chosen a body to possess that day, then he had chosen the body of that young man who wanted nothing more than to make an anti-confession, to espouse tired, bigoted beliefs.

The priest recovered enough to say, "I'm afraid this is neither the time nor the place for you, my son."

"What do you mean, 'time or place'?"

"It's 2001."

"So?"

"So, it's the 21st century. Attitudes have changed. A lot's changing."

"A lot may be changing," I said, "but for every action there's an equal or greater reaction. A *greater* reaction. A blowback. You think what I believe is old news? Think again. We'll still be talking about this twenty, thirty years from now. There will *always* be me."

"You got the wrong church, kid," said the priest. "Maybe twenty years ago, but now...If you refuse to take responsibility for your sins, then I must ask you to leave this place of worship."

"You refuse," I said, my voice rising, "to hear my sins? My brother's sins are my own! *I* take responsibility for his wrongdoing."

"Take responsibility for your own wrongdoing," said the priest. "Are you your brother?"

"We're twins," I all but screamed. The priest made a move to rise. I stayed him with my voice alone. "Identical, the same in every way, in *everything*. If you were me, you'd understand. Because of him I feel things I shouldn't be feeling, and *that's* a sin."

"You don't know what a sin is," the priest said, his face pressed to the mesh screen. "What you've come here for today has nothing to do with sin, nothing to do with God, with Jesus Christ, with goodness, nothing to do with faith and everything to do with your own personal problems with your brother. He's your twin, huh. God makes even twins different. Everyone is unique—"

"They shouldn't be," I said. "We should all be the same— but only the right same. The right kind of same. Same in desires, same in beliefs, in how we think, in who we follow, in who we worship, in who we love, in who we live around, in who—"

"Get out. I will not tolerate you using our religion for your own ends."

"But I gave first communion here."

"You were never confirmed. Now leave. Go join that drunk Melvin in the mountains."

I drove back to L.A. that night. For the next three weeks, I searched as the nation searched for those responsible. I was not responsible. Jeremy was, but not me, never Stan Pangborn. If my brother had not been born.... But Jeremy had come into this world trailing after me. He had clutched, kicked, wailed. Tried to drag me back, then down. At that time, when we were young, I could not succeed. In the wake of the attack on America, I could.

I sought out smaller religions, the no-name sects that operated under the umbrella of generalized Christianity. Born-agains gone rogue, a new theology. I found them on the outskirts of L.A., underground and in abandoned buildings and in tract homes. Found them in the high desert, in cities like Lancaster, Tehachapi, and on the way to Vegas: Victorville, Barstow, Baker. Everywhere I showed up, I heard talk of the enemy within our borders, sinners in New York who had brought this punishment on the heads of good people, the good righteous true American people, by choosing to live in sin. The president was soft. He talked tough, the cowboy in the White House who wanted the evil mastermind dead or alive, but until the entire Middle East was nuked he held no sway in their eyes. Jesus fared no better. Christ himself was weak, not even a man. He was wrong to preach forgiveness, tolerance, love of one's neighbor. There would be no love, for love led to terrorism. Only the sword would do. Jesus could be forgiven for not understanding since he lived in an ancient time. If he lived now, Christ would carry not a cross on his back but an assault rifle slung over his shoulder, across his bare chest two bandoliers packed with enough ammunition to take out a church, and he would be a Man. He would understand his place in this world—and fall in line.

I wanted to believe, my desire to believe the most dangerous weapon of all.

I attended Sunday services inside dead factories and squat buildings that stretched behind ill-watered lawns. I attended a super-Sunday-morning-whip-up-the-crowd worship service in a former hog-slaughtering warehouse near the entrance to Mojave. The preacher stood at the podium dressed in army fatigues, sported America's Rifle and delivered a stunning remix of the Book of Revelations. Eternal war was at hand; the Four Horsemen stalked the cities alongside the Seven Deadly Sins; only here, in the desert, were the faithful safe. As the preacher thundered on, images flashed across a jumbotron screen positioned behind him, a substitute for the looming crucified Christ ubiquitous in the churches of my former religion.

"There is no going back from this," the preacher boomed. "We may be forever fearful now, but we are also forever enraged, forever at the ready, forever willing to get our hands dirty if it means having the freedom to do as we please and the ability to crush *all* our enemies. Every single enemy, even those we may not see as enemies now.

"Satan has shown himself and his works, but to combat the evil, God will send His Only Son into our midst in the form of a warrior, a brute, a leader, a take-no-prisoners scoundrel who tells it like it is and doesn't care if he breaks the laws and upends society to return order and righteousness to this country. Now when the Only Son will appear, I know not. But soon, I believe. Soon."

The preacher held up the Bible and cried out, "This remains the Good Book, but I believe it's in need of some fine tuning, a revision. A new way of looking at God's Word. God's Word is whatever *we* say it is." He opened to Leviticus 20:13, Romans 1:26, and targeted those directly responsible for the attack on America. In triumph, the preacher raised his assault rifle. "They didn't have these back then. But Christ would gladly take up one of these against those enemies and pursue the penalty we all know is just."

At first, I was entranced. But after the third month of meetings, after the preacher at the former hog-slaughtering warehouse promised our congregation the appearance of a military vehicle at the following week's service, and that military vehicle never did appear (we were told it had been sent to the Middle East); after the same images flashed on the jumbotron, and the same passages were read from that good book with no outward results, no immediate bloodshed, I felt something I never thought I would: boredom. Boredom was the worst feeling; I loathed feeling bored. I was not alone. So many in the congregation felt the dreaded sense of listlessness as well. They itched for the action, they itched for the entertainment, they itched for the star who would lead them out of the desert and into prime time. The Only Son did not appear as soon as the preacher had promised; it would be well over a decade before he did. None of these small sects were for me, I realized on the last day I would ever attend service in the former hog-slaughtering warehouse. That day, after the sermon had ended, I followed the preacher to his office and asked him for the name of his church.

"Well," the preacher began. Then, seeing I wanted an

answer, he continued: "We call it, uh, The Church of the Overpowering."

"The name's cool. Still…. How many members does it have? Seems like there's way more money in the aisles than members."

"It's not good to ask these questions."

"Just tell me. Please."

"What's your name, son?"

"Stan."

The preacher's jaw dropped. He cocked his head to one side in the form of a question mark. He asked me to repeat my name. When I did, he said, "Oh, *Stan*. I apologize. I heard, uh, something different."

I waited. Each second I stood there, I had more and more trouble containing my irritation.

At last the preacher said, "All you need to know is our numbers are growing. Now let me ask you a question, *Stan*: Are you a spy working for the deepest reaches of our nation's government?"

"No. I'm a 22-year-old office worker from L.A."

The preacher pointed to the door. "That may be true," he said, and he brought up his assault rifle from behind the desk, "in which case I'll give you a chance to get back to that big city of sin now or else risk falling victim to a terrible accident on these premises.

"The desert is wide and open," he said as I left.

I never returned to that part of California. The faithful there could have their desert. They were on such unsure footing, and I had exposed their insecurities wholesale. I could never be a part of such weakness. But an established, official religion, a strong, virile, truly growing outfit would have to welcome me, for I looked and behaved like one of them. I would make sure I fit the part of what they idealized. And I would not give up on those responsible.

One night in the sixth month of the new era, early spring, I was blessed with a vision in which I witnessed firsthand the towers burning. My vision was television footage, the news channel PNN, and that Tuesday morning in September played out as it had in our waking lives. But by the end of the vision, instead of both towers falling, I saw only one. One tower remained standing.

Five

Wednesday, July 1st, one in the afternoon, just as we'd agreed. Seated on my couch, going through a photo album, I heard their knock. I let them in before returning to the album. Photos of the Pangborn Twins as infants above the baptismal font. Photos of Stan and Jeremy at the age of three taking a bath together. Photos of Frank and Linda holding hands.

I closed the album before either missionary could see inside.

"Taking a trip down memory lane?" This from Raybury.

"When we were a family," I said, "we were a good family. Happy."

"When did that change?" Brannigan asked.

"The summer we graduated high school. My brother came out that summer. My father left us shortly after that."

"Because of your brother?"

"Of course. It had to be because of him. My father did so much throughout our lives to make things perfect, and what Jeremy did was a betrayal. Dad had to leave."

"I'm sorry," said Brannigan. Both missionaries remained standing. They let their backpacks drop to the carpet, as if in preparation for something.

Raybury spoke up. "You probably didn't pray then, but you can pray now. Pray that your family stays happy, even if they're apart."

I issued a harsh, ugly snort. "We can never be happy if we're apart."

"What's wrong, Stan?" Brannigan moved closer to me. "You're different from the first time we met."

"I'm no different."

"You seem...even angrier."

"Dangerous," added Raybury. "Did you read? Did you pray?"

"Yes and yes." I pressed my fingertips to my temples. "I got nothing."

"You will get something, in time. Right now it's because you're new to our faith."

"Fuck your faith," I said. "I'm not new to it. I read those passages. I prayed. *Nothing* happened."

Brannigan lunged toward the couch, grappled me, clutched my throat and pushed my head into the pillow so that I could not save my own life (*his* life), and Brannigan, with the full fury of the Manifested, his people (*our* people), their shared persecution, that tragic sense of history mixed with the land, the great Southwest, Louisiana to Arizona, Gila monsters and Apache, the sun and sky and hope, bullets in the bodies of their leaders, migration and, later, reconciliation with a government that had once shunned them; acceptance, pride—

(I understood then: here were men who would use the mistakes of their past to consolidate their future.)

—with all this quaking in his voice, Brannigan said, "Stan Pangborn, listen!"

It was not his voice but the voice of Another.

I felt Raybury holding my legs and was shocked at the strength of these two young men. I could hear my phone buzzing, and after the buzzing ceased, I was struck with the most savage headache of my life. I slipped and fought back, squinted like an ant under a magnifying sun.

"Listen, listen, listen," Brannigan breathed into my ear.

Raybury spoke in another language—not even a language, tongues. I remembered that day at the Devil's Punchbowl, holding Jeremy's hand—and where was my brother, my sister, now? With me, always with me. That was my way out. I would not hold him forever.

"Believe in our savior," Brannigan commanded. "Believe Invincible Father can save you."

"I—"

Brannigan struck me across the face with his palm. I stared at him, shocked, my eyes welling. He raised his hand again.

"What the fuck?" I said. "That's assault!"

"It's our way," said Brannigan, and he struck me again, this time even harder. One side of my face stung from his blows.

"I'll put it into you," Brannigan spat. "I'll put it into you!"

"Put what into me?"

Raybury continued to speak in tongues.

"You are going to be a Man, Stan, if I have to hit you one hundred, two hundred, three thousand, four million times."

"Okay! Okay! Just don't—"

Again: the palm, the blow, my face. I could not defend myself. My ears rang with Raybury's nonsense words. What I heard sapped my strength, neutralized my arms. Brannigan struck thrice more, and with each attack I cried out. But each time I cried out I felt my voice strengthening, my mind settling itself on the future, my anger magnified but at last focused. It felt good to be one of them.

I no longer hurt. I stretched out fully and watched as Brannigan let his arm drop. He knelt beside the couch and opened the Book of the Manifested, which he placed on my stomach. Raybury had ceased his gibberish and now knelt beside his companion. Together these missionaries prayed for me, of all people.

"Stan Pangborn! By the authority of The Leader and Invincible Father Himself, we hurt you to heal you, to redirect your anger and despair away from The Church, your Friend, and instead at those who deserve that anger and despair, which will not go to waste in this world. In the name of the Church of the Manifested in all its glory, amen."

"Stan Pangborn," Raybury echoed. "By the authority of the Max Manifested, I too bless you to redirect your suffering so that it falls squarely on our enemies. Invincible Father, Mighty Father, You know Stan can easily be Manifested. Just look at him. Stan thinks he's alone, cast out, but You will gladly take him. He will no longer know loneliness, the greatest disease. Cure Stan Pangborn of his disease. Bless him in Your Invincible Name, amen!"

"Amen," I said, the word slipping off my tongue like a secret.

The missionaries lifted their hands off my body and stood to watch me. I closed my eyes. For a time, I flitted in and out of consciousness. In darkness, I was witness to countless eyes widening and flickering, passing judgment, the faces of friends and almost-lovers I'd left behind. Main Street Anomar, the one true; Jeremy in a princess dress at a Halloween party, smiling, waving his hand; a family gathered around for a festive holiday dinner; unnamed, unborn sisters and brothers, mothers and fathers; and later, possibly only seconds later, I opened my eyes and knew that any lingering doubt had died.

I sat up, touched my chest, my head. Raybury and Brannigan continued to observe. Each held open their Book of the Manifested. Outside, a few guys passed my apartment building on the way to the beach. Their voices drifted through the open slider then dwindled to silence. Only the ocean's voice remained.

"What just happened?" I asked.

"Something beautiful," Brannigan answered.

"Simone and I had a big fight yesterday. I think we might break up—if we haven't already."

Raybury asked if I wanted to break up.

"If she had an open mind then maybe not.... I've always been open to trying new things, experimentation, you know. As it stands now, I don't know if we're the perfect match. She's hot, but she's probably not my, you know, Perfect. I just don't see how we can be together if she's not willing to try this out with me."

Raybury leaned forward. "Dude," he said, "if this world were perfect, if *women* were perfect, couples would stay together. Families would stay together."

"But that's not the world we live in," Brannigan said.

"Invincible Father knows this world. He understands right now the struggles men face when dealing with women and anybody else who's different or doesn't agree. That's why right now we're not fully Manifested—what we call 'Max Manifested.'"

"That's when you make it on The List," I said.

"That's right. The List. The Manifest."

Raybury cleared his throat. "We're told perfection doesn't exist, that there's no perfect guy. We don't buy that. Perfection *does* exist. Men *can* be perfect. Just look at Invincible Father. He used to be on earth, in this world, one of us, trying like us to be perfect. Through His complete and Invincible Faith, and His strength and attitude, He succeeded. He no longer fails. He doesn't experience breakups. He doesn't go through divorces. His women never leave Him. Anything His family wants, He gives them."

"And He gets anything He wants from them," Brannigan said. "Anything."

"That's great," I said. "But...doesn't that happen only in the afterlife? Not this world?"

"It *can* happen in this world. It *should* happen in this world."

"It *will* happen in this world." Brannigan offered up the Book of the Manifested. "It's all here," he said. "How this world will be."

"Only a man and a woman can be married," I said, my eyes locked with theirs. "An actual man and an actual woman."

"That's correct, Stan. Women were made for men, after all."

"The young Manifested man searches for his Perfect, and

once he finds her he works on her until she's convinced to join."

"Also correct."

"But during that time sex is withheld."

"Not necessarily," Brannigan said. "Sex is very important to the Manifested way. We don't say no to sex before marriage, but the man must be in control. He must be the one to call the shots. It's his choice, not hers."

"And it better be with the right chick," said Raybury.

"It's very important, Stan," Brannigan said, "that as a man you know you have a much greater burden than your Perfect. That's how it is in this world. Men have it worse, they just do. Women can fail—they're allowed to fail, they're expected to fail, they will continue to fail—but men must be perfect in this world, so they can achieve Invincibility in the next."

I told the missionaries I had never been clear on what happened after death. Brannigan and Raybury explained that in the afterlife, The Invincible Fortress, as CotM called it, men could reach the level of Invincible Father Himself. In the afterlife, once-mortal men could become Invincible themselves and be granted whatever they desired.

"Anything," said Raybury. "Anything you wanted in your former life, here on earth, you can have in The Invincible Fortress."

"Anything?"

"Anything your heart, your mind, your spirit desires."

"What about your body?" I asked. "What your *body* desires..."

"Even the most sinful things in this world are allowed in The Invincible Fortress," Brannigan revealed. "You're allowed them if you're a man and your name is on The Manifest."

"It's actually good to be a man," I said, surprised. "The most sinful things…"

"The most sinful thoughts," Brannigan said. "We know all men have them. Nothing is too out there for The Church. If it's wrong in this world, this country, it's right in The Invincible Fortress."

"So many constraints," I muttered.

"Look who runs the world," Raybury said.

"And who runs this country," added Brannigan. "But, you see, Stan, it's the ultimate reward for what you go through in this life to achieve perfection and make it onto The Manifest. Invincible Father understands this life is not easy, it's not easy to be a man, so He's more than happy to reward you for your perseverance and faith. He wants The Invincible Fortress to be the ultimate paradise, where all your wishes and desires will be fulfilled, no matter who's with you."

"It could be your family," Raybury said, "but it doesn't have to be. It could be…well, your mistress, or several mistresses. Whatever makes you happy."

"You earned it," Brannigan said. "For sticking with the Church of the Manifested. For sticking with Invincible Father and following His orders."

"Awesome," I said. "Just so, so awesome."

"I take it you're in."

"I welcome everything I've heard."

What I did not tell these missionaries: I had for much of my life seen religion as my way out. Lately, I had seen the Church of the Manifested as both the excuse and the escape. The information I'd just heard confirmed my belief. I thought of my father and perfectionism, his masculine front of posturing and preening. I thought of Simone and the idea that

I too could become a god in the afterlife, the beauty of failure nullified, the security I would possess and the control I would wield.

"Jeremy. My twin—my identical twin brother." I held up the Book of the Manifested. "I don't suppose there's any room for him in this, is there."

Brannigan delivered his words by rote. "The Church is working on that, Stan. Obviously things have changed. We're in a different time now. Doctrine can change, even in CotM. We used to be not as accepting."

"But still not accepting of trans people."

"Right. When it comes to trans...that's just..."

Brannigan rarely looked to Raybury for support, but he did now. The younger missionary spoke up. "We just don't see the 'T' in LGBTQ ever becoming part of the Manifested."

"What your brother is going through," said Brannigan, "is not part of Invincible Father's plan."

"Because it's a sin," I pressed. "A major failure that could be avoided."

"Yes," Raybury said. "We're not alone. It's not just religion, Stan. It's a lot of other places, people, groups—they all feel the way we do."

"People in power," Brannigan said. "That's key."

"If I'm going to continue with this," I said. "I have to confess something. Does the Church of the Manifested hear confessions?"

"Of course, Stan. We'd hear the devil confess if he was willing."

I took to the edge of the couch, balanced there, my hands wringing in my lap for added effect.

"One day when we were kids," I said, "he walked in on—"

—Come forward to childhood, brother, and do not despise it because it is small and it is little.

And do not turn away greatnesses in some parts from the smallnesses, I countered, for the smallnesses are known from the greatnesses.

—Now you're thinking, Stan. I'll take over.

No you won't.

—I damn well will, Stan. Let go!

Ah shit! That hurts.

—Will you?

Yes, okay. Yes. Just: don't make anything up.

—I walked in on him, Stan, my brother. We were thirteen, it was after school and Frank and Linda weren't home. I went into Stan's room without knocking because it was my turn to have the Super Nintendo and he'd kept it one more day than he should have. I walked in. And when I opened the door I saw Stan Pangborn almost completely naked. It was like seeing myself naked at thirteen. Almost naked. Stan stood in front of his dresser mirror wearing panties—Linda's panties. Must have been Mom's. He'd snuck them from her dresser into his own.

Stan jumped back as I stayed standing in the doorway. My mouth hung open. My brother cupped his genitals. "What the fuck are you doing?" he said. "What the fuck are *you* doing?" I questioned back. Stan screamed at me to get out, get out. His face was fever red. He swallowed his shock and embarrassment at being discovered—and what he vomited was rage. His eyes flashed murder. I backed up. He advanced toward me. "Get out!" he shrieked again. I laughed then—laughed at the sight of my brother menacing me while wearing only a pair of our mother's panties. The laughter set

Stan off. His eyes broke wide like yolks in a pan, and in a low voice said, "Nasty fucker. *Nasty fucker.* Let's fuck. You wanna fuck? Let's fuck." I told Stan to stop, and when he grabbed me I told him to let go, stop saying those words. He wouldn't stop. I was crying from the shock and fear. My brother hadn't changed. I remembered the playground at Gordon Lawrence, the games of king of the hill and smear-the-queer, and how my brother and I fought each other to avoid being called out as the weakest. Those days he would have the upper hand, I would fall backward off the hill, I was the one to be smeared, and this was like that. He held me by the throat, shook me, pressed me against the wall beside his door. I was choking. He would kill me then for what I'd discovered.

That's enough, Jer.

—You don't deny it.

I don't. I would have killed you that day.

—But. I slammed my fist upward, connected with the elbow of Stan's outstretched arm. We both heard the snap. He let go and I ran out of his room and down the hall. Stan chased me, tackled me. We fought; I let him beat me. I laughed as he struck me again and again because he remained in Mom's underwear. My brother, who was already fronting macho, like Frank, exposed now. I should have fled the house—I'm certain he would have chased me outside and then everyone on our street would have witnessed the truth. They'd all know—

THAT IS ENOUGH, JER.

—Over to you, brother. I've said my piece. For now.

Brannigan and Raybury looked as if they'd been asked to dive headfirst into a well. "Why tell us this, Stan?" Brannigan asked.

"If I'm going to convert and be on my way to Max Manifestation, I needed to tell you that. So there are no surprises."

"I mean," said Raybury, "when I was in high school my friends and I shot a music video and one of them wore a dress. He was still my friend."

"This is different," Brannigan said. "I think that's what Stan's trying to tell us. This goes against the teachings of CotM. Was that the only time?"

"Yes," I convinced them. "Just that one—"

—You sure about that, Stan?

The missionaries gave me a curious look. "Just that one time," I continued. "I was experimenting, that's all."

"You were young," Brannigan reasoned. "CotM welcomes you, and we're glad you told us."

"Thank you," I said. "I...I hurt my brother that day, and that wasn't the only day. I hurt him many days after. I was... very physical with him. He'd hurt me, so I felt the need to hurt him. That afternoon he was so hysterical from my tormenting he called my dad who warned me, what little good that did. Another afternoon, Jeremy ran out of the house screaming, and I chased him for a while before I gave up."

"You had clothes on that time, I hope."

All three of us laughed. "Yes," I said. "Clothes from then on."

—The truth, Stan. Tell the—

"I have a lot of anger in me," I said. "I...I don't think I'm a good person. Some people I knew used to tell me I'm not even a person."

"That's terrible, Stan. We feel for you." Brannigan pointed to the Book of the Manifested I held. "You think you can't join us on the path to perfection, but you can. You can definitely be one of us. Eventually, you will be Max Manifested."

"It doesn't matter if you're not a good person," said Raybury. "What matters to CotM is that you want to join us. You want to be on The Manifest."

"I do. Desperately."

"Look at you. You look like us. We would never turn you away. So you did some bad things when you were a teenager."

"Boys will be boys," Brannigan said.

"Boys will be boys," echoed Raybury.

Brannigan took up the torch. "You're not the best, but that's nothing new, Stan. So many guys aren't the best. Your sins are small potatoes compared to what others have done."

"Even Hitler is on The Manifest," Raybury admitted.

"*Hitler joined the Church of the Manifested?*"

"He did join The Church," Brannigan said. "Just not when he was alive."

"You can join CotM when you're dead?"

"Every man does," said Brannigan. "The Church finds all the dead dudes. If you're a man, any man, you're guaranteed a chance at making it onto The Manifest."

"But Hitler was pure evil."

"The worst evil," Raybury said. "We don't deny that. But when we baptize the dead by proxy we don't pass judgment. We don't judge—we leave that up to Our Invincible Father. I mean there's Hitler, but we've also baptized great figures in history too, like George Washington, Ronald Reagan…"

"The good and the bad," Brannigan said. "It's all for Invincible Father to decide."

"I see," I said. "So even a mass murderer…"

"*Any* man, Stan. Any man. They'll face Invincible Father in the world to come."

"What about...What about somebody who's still alive but they're a murderer? Could that person join the Church of the Manifested?"

The missionaries paused to consider. Raybury looked to Brannigan to handle this one. The older missionary said, "It would be a man, right?"

"Yes," I said. "A true, natural man."

"This man could," Brannigan said. "His conversion would be difficult, and it would take time..."

"The numbers are more important," said Raybury. To Brannigan: "I think it's okay I said that, right?"

Brannigan looked only slightly chagrined. He said, "The numbers are more important than the person."

"The numbers?"

"We need those numbers. Fill the quota." He and Raybury laughed. "It's a joke among us missionaries. So, you see, Stan, it could be anyone. We just need the numbers, the men, and then from them the girls, their Perfects. Even a murderer can find his Perfect, you know."

"And he can be baptized in this world?" I asked. "Eventually?"

Brannigan took a deep breath, exhaled. "Murder is one of the very worst sins a man can commit. That person would have to go directly to Phoenix, to the CotM Center, confess, repent..."

"But if you truly repent," Raybury said, "and talk to The Leader willfully, truthfully, then you should be forgiven at baptism."

Brannigan nodded. "Baptism would not be for...many months."

"Thanks," I said. "Knowing there are others worse than me out there helps."

"There's always somebody worse," said Raybury.

There's always somebody better.

"To better your chances at making The List," Brannigan said, "you can read that book in your hands, and you can also work on your brother."

"My sister."

"Fine. Talk to her about what happened between you two. Tell her you're sorry for what you did. Sorry for the abuse you put her through."

"I'm afraid," I admitted. "Afraid I'd find out things about myself, by talking to her."

"Maybe you need to find out those things. Only then will you be a Man."

"Try for CotM," said Raybury. "Try for Invincible Father. Try for your family."

I told Brannigan and Raybury I didn't have a family.

Yet, I thought.

Brannigan said, "The wickedness of any man, every one of any man's sins, can be forgiven if only he joins the One True Church."

"I'm afraid I won't find my Perfect."

"Don't fear, Stan."

"You don't understand," I said. "I'm afraid she won't...stick with me. What I'm saying is...what if...what if sex is a problem?"

Brannigan asked why sex would be a problem for someone like me.

"I can't give up control, but that's what my girlfriend wants me to do. She says I have to give up control to truly love her."

"Not true," said Brannigan. "The Church of the Manifested teaches that all men can have complete control and still have a true, loving connection with their women."

"Women actually do want to be completely controlled," Raybury said. "Many of them just don't know it yet."

"The problem with sex," I said, "is you have to lose yourself in someone else, and that scares me. I can't give up that much of myself. If I do, I think I'd be my sister then."

"Just know," Brannigan said, "in the Invincible Fortress, there are no problems when it comes to sex. The messiness of this world doesn't exist in the afterlife. All men are satisfied, and they in turn satisfy."

"And there's no more fear. Or failure."

"Correct, Stan."

We arranged to hold our third Manly Talk before the Invincible Meeting on Sunday, July 5th. I would attend the meeting after our talk. We would finish up the rest of the Manly Talks the following week, when the missionaries' schedule was more open. Together, the three of us prayed to Invincible Father, a prayer for Stan Pangborn and one for his brother, now his sister, may Jeri Pangborn reach an understanding of her own.

And through this, I smiled.

THE PLANE TILTED to the left and I snapped my eyes open, expecting the wing to fall off. When it didn't, I sucked in the recycled compartment air and held my breath. Watching Stan Pangborn exhale, the man next to me said, "You ever think about taking classes?"

"I'm sorry. What classes?"

"Classes to get rid of that fear of flying."

Aware now of how tightly I was gripping the armrests, I raised my arms, flicked my wrists to get the circulation back, and faced my fellow passenger.

"I took 'em," the man said. "No shame in it. My wife and I went to the Cayman Islands back in April, and the first thing I said to the stewardess before we took off was 'Let's roll.'"

"I'll think about it," I said.

"If you're scared, don't think about the crash in Buffalo. Think about the Hudson River one, where everyone survived."

If we were passing over a body of water, it would be too small to land in. Desert stretched in all directions. No Sully, I thought.

On my left, reclining as far back as her aisle seat would allow, a woman had not opened her eyes since popping a pill prior to take-off.

"What are you headed to Phoenix for?" the man asked.

"Research," I said.

"You a scientist?"

"Of a sort. I'm interested in religion. I study it, like a scientist. I figured I'd check out the Center."

"Ah. The Church of the Manifested."

"Are you a member?"

The man shook his head. "Nah. I know about it, though. Most Phoenicians do."

"Phoenicians," I said. "I feel like I'm headed to ancient Egypt."

We heard a bing, the fasten seatbelt sign flashed, and the captain announced we would be making our final descent shortly.

"You're not too far off," the man offered. "Arizona's first governor's buried in a pyramid in the city."

"No way."

"Governor Hunt. Him and his wife. It's a small pyramid, but you can see it from a distance."

"I'll check it out."

"Try not to spend all your time at the Center."

"Have you been there?"

As an answer, the man smiled, leaned back, and closed his eyes.

SHE WAS STANDING beside the appropriate baggage carousel wearing a hooded pullover, burgundy corduroys, Converse sneakers and a pale shirt with a picture of Elliott Smith on the front. Looking at her for the first time in years, she reminded me of a badly drawn boy. I approached. She unfolded her arms and took a few steps forward as if afraid to fall. We met underneath the American flag.

"Erin," I said.

"Stan," she said.

We embraced, the strength of her hug far more forceful than mine, my fingers on the square of her back so that I felt her spine, the raised ridge of bones running down her back like a set of dragon scales. I wanted to sweep my fingers down her back and force in those bones, one by one, such was the surprise I felt then. I had never touched Erin before, and I was suddenly deadened and weary in the way I often was when greeting people from my past.

Her full name was Erin Anne Masterson. In college she was a self-avowed straight edge; nearly a decade later, she still looked the part. That day at Sky Harbor I was unaware she saw me as more than a friend; to her, I was an excuse not to sub, a possibility, a future.

She took her glasses off and cleaned the lenses with the edge of her shirt. I had only my backpack with me, so we bypassed the luggage carousel and wound our way through the crowds eager to escape; if any who saw us assumed we were more than friends, they would have been dead wrong. She walked ahead and I ambled along obediently like a misbegotten stork unable to find its way out of the burning marsh.

Certain things Erin did not like about herself, and so she kept her distance face-forward as if people passing by would pick up those things the way clothing collects lint. She did not like her height (5'2"), she did not like her skin peppered with acne running along her cheeks (all the more embarrassing because she was 31 years old). She did not like her lips she saw as too heavy, nor her glasses she saw as too thick, nor her feet that to her felt like two bricks stolen from the base of the Statue of Liberty and left in a closet to be forgotten.

—Jesus, Stan. You're laying it on thick here, wouldn't you say.

Shut it, Jer. Jeri. I'm writing a book here.

—So presumptuous about so many people for so long.

I said shut it. Go write your own book.

If only you could pass on your faults to others as one would a virus, then be done with it and happy.

Erin drove a beat-up old hatchback. The air conditioning was faulty, but seeing as it was November in Phoenix and only 79 degrees out, we would survive. I kept my backpack at my feet. The interior smelled like fast food, yet I saw no wrappers. At my feet, along with my backpack, were cracked CD cases containing The Pixies, The Smiths, Belle & Sebastian.

The hatchback accelerated up the on-ramp rabbit quick. Erin kept her hands on the wheel ten and two. On this day, Sunday, and at this time, 12:15 in the afternoon, the freeway was flowing. I saw bumper stickers that spoke of the past, present, future. We were still a few years out from the gargantuan American flags on the back of pickup trucks.

"If it's all right with you," I said, "I'd like to go to the Center today, if it's not too hot out later."

"It won't get too hot out. Phoenix is livable this time of year."

"What do you do the other parts of the year?"

"I don't know yet. Remember: I only moved here at the end of September."

"That's right."

"Convenient for you."

"I'm glad I hit you up."

"I'm glad you did too."

Another thing she disliked: her voice, which to her sounded like a 90-year-old trying to speak through a blown-up balloon.

—You disliked, Stan. *You* disliked. Just because she wasn't the ideal—

In the hatchback and through lunch, our conversation was intermittent at best. Every topic I turned on myself, every question I asked for my benefit. Unaware, even at age 30, of how self-serving I sounded, I engaged Erin with what I thought were the best stories from our mutual college experience and my life in L.A.

—Now you're admitting some truth.

I know. I have that capacity. The more I talked the less Erin felt comfortable with what she saw. There was something a little off about Stan Pangborn. He had a way of talking to you without actually talking to you. More like talking *at* you. But she had not had a friend visit since moving to the Valley of the Sun, had not carried on a face-to-face conversation with any friends in several months, and so, since loneliness is the worst disease of all, she let the nitpickiness go for now.

I paused, the pause turned into a lull, the lull turned on us and became a full-fledged Awkward Silence, and Erin took this opportunity to ask about my family.

"Family." I gave intense attention to my plate. "It was a family. It's just scattered people now."

"I didn't know you were having problems."

"Because of my brother, mostly. Dad and Linda divorced. As soon as we graduated it was like, no more obligations here."

"That happens."

"A son coming out to his parents and his identical twin brother? Maybe…"

"No, I mean parents waiting until their children have graduated before separating."

"Divorcing."

"Right."

"Where's your brother now?" Erin asked.

"Austin. He was in New York, but then his, you know, partner got some position at the University of Texas. Something in graphic design, the university's webmaster or something. So they moved to Texas together, and they've been living there ever since."

"He was in New York for a while."

"Yeah."

"He never once visited you at college? Or any time after you got out of high school?"

"Never."

"I've never seen him," Erin said.

"You don't need to. He looks just like me."

"Still…. Do you have a picture of him on your phone?"

"I don't keep any pictures of Jeremy anywhere." I paused for effect. "You raise a child for, what, almost twenty years and then *that* happens? And she *supports* him coming out? How *could* Dad stay with her?"

"Stan, what are you talking about? Didn't this happen a long time ago?"

"Twelve years ago," I specified. "That's not that long a time, really. I've tried to figure it out in other ways. I went to these churches, lots of little ones, in the last several years, since 9/11, and I know none of them are right for me. It has to be a big, established religion. It's gotta be CotM. The Church of the Manifested."

Later, we stood on a corner across from CenterPost, Erin with her arms crossed, her mouth a flatline, I intent on writing observations down in my compact spiral-bound notebook. She asked me what I was writing.

"Just my thoughts on being here. I can't believe I'm finally here."

—Why, she thought.

Don't get into her head now.

—You can but I can't? Give me my due, Stan.

Fine. Have at it.

—How generous of you, Stanley. Erin wasn't denying divorce was painful. She understood the hardship. Her parents had realized their mistake only after years of arguing had passed. During the arguments, Erin took shelter in other rooms and imagined herself as someone who could easily escape what she endured because she was famous—not rich—for having done something bold, brave, something no one else had done before. President. She understood Stan's parents' divorce was traumatic, but still: 30 was a far cry from 18, and besides, Stan was a guy. He should've moved on by now.

At least I *felt* something, unlike you...

—I felt plenty, brother. Now, back to you...

We wandered through the outer sanctum of CenterPost. I walked ahead like my father, and Erin trailed behind at a distance, the true purpose and intensity of my visit dawning on her with more and more light. As we walked, she lost ground to me. I forgot she was there, forgot she'd picked me up at the airport and agreed to put me up for three nights. *Three nights*, she thought, *and he's here for the Manifested. What a bummer.*

At one point I stopped to take in the statue of Conrad Tolson. Martyred in Louisiana in the struggle for religious freedom in the first decade of the 20th century, CT was said to have had a twin brother who'd died in infancy, never named.

Erin and I entered the Center Interior. A multi-level building the size of at least three Grand Hyatt hotels, this place would happily consume me in its many rooms and hallways, and I would never reemerge. At the visitor's post, we signed up for a guided tour of the premises. During that tour, a studious Stan Pangborn took notes.

Our guide, a girl Manifested, asked what I was writing.

"Just the facts, miss."

"Are you a reporter? A journalist?"

"I'm a marketer."

Our guide smiled, her eyes fixated on my notebook.

Erin whispered to me, "I want to know what you're writing."

I showed her. Dates I'd found engraved on the bases of statues. Names and mottoes, scraps of history. I sought to capture all this for the future—a future that had yet to materialize fully in my mind, but at least I could no longer fault myself for being unaware and uneducated. As I listened and learned, I no longer felt my brother as I had before, nor would I ever again fall in line with the detractors who adhered to all manner of stereotypes and speculation. Manifested men are all misogynists, Manifested women are desperate and malleable. I embraced my newfound knowledge as I would my future child.

At the conclusion of the tour, our guide, armed with pamphlets, attempted to continue the conversation. I glanced at Erin, at last acknowledged her disengagement, and begged off further information for now.

In the hatchback, Erin said, "You want to go back there."

"I have to. There's still a lot more to learn."

She was about to say, You're not going to convert, are you? but kept her mouth shut instead. Years of awkward social interactions had taught her to ask only the right questions.

"I'll drop you off tomorrow morning. You can make a day of it."

"I don't want to ignore you."

Yeah, right, Erin thought.

"It's okay. I need to take a sub job anyway. Gotta get my hours for the credential."

"How's that going?"

"It's going."

Later, on the first night, the second night, the third night, Erin would say, "I'm going to change now," or "I'm going to bed now," and leave the bedroom door open for Stan, who would remain on the couch, the TV flickering, the notebook and pen in his hands. On these nights Erin's voice sounded even thinner than usual. She'd been beaten down, weary of putting up with Stan Pangborn's self-interest. Each day I'd gone to the Center, and in the evening we'd gone out to eat, engaged in fitful conversation, then retired to her apartment to watch a movie or two.

She asked me, on the final night, "Are you going to join them?"

"I'm never going to join them. But I need to know what makes them *them*. There's a lot I admire about them. A lot. They're not going away. And there's my brother. Jeremy needs to talk to them."

"It's 2009, Stan. Don't you think—"

"I just found out my brother is going to be my sister."

"So he's—"

"Planning to transition. I just found out. That's why this visit is so important."

"Stan..." Erin sighed. "What you think is a big deal isn't really all that big a deal."

I gritted my teeth as I spoke: "Tell that to—"

"I just don't think it works that way, Stan."

"What doesn't work what way?"

"I don't think your brother becomes your sister when he transitions."

"What does he become then?"

"Whatever he wants to be. It's up to him to decide, not you. It just sounds offensive, the way you say it. But you're right about one thing."

"What?"

"You'll probably find sympathetic ears in the Church of the Manifested."

Eager, I showed Erin the notes and photos I'd taken, and still she feared. I told her about the subsequent tours I'd gone on, the questions I'd posed, the facts I'd received. Her concern did not vacate. Awareness and sadness intertwined and gripped her. The end of intimacy, of touch, of direct eye contact. Was this her future, with every man? Was the Church of the Manifested the future?

Erin drove me to Sky Harbor on the morning of our fourth day together. The hatchback was silent, its occupants unmoving. After she pulled up curbside, we exchanged a quick goodbye and I exited without looking back. Erin, for her part, did not linger.

Weeks after I'd returned to L.A. and my career in marketing, I received an email from Erin. In it she apologized for avoiding me and not taking an interest in what captivated me. She admitted she was surprised I had not made a move on her. I hadn't been interested in sex—*but isn't that what you're supposed to do when you travel a long way to visit a friend?* she wrote.

Without responding, I deleted her message. Never again would we communicate in any way.

Six

I believed.

I believed the Second Civil War would be fought over a period of many years. It would be fought by soldiers, by civilians, by soldiers dressed as civilians, civilians dressed as soldiers. Officers of laws no longer upheld or even in existence. The battlefield would range from Bangor, Maine to the backwoods of San Diego's North County. Hundreds of thousands of lives would be lost in a matter of days. Bodies would be dumped in mass graves. Entire suburbs would be wiped out, and every social platform and site and podcast and channel and station would provide 24-hour continuous coverage. It would be impossible to tell foe from friend. Countries all over the world would lend their support and contribute to the downfall of these Once-United States. Citizens of all ages and races and orientations would fight for their religion or for the absence of religion, for their sexuality and the right to express it or for the right to deny others the right to express it, and they would die having finally felt the beating heart of our mighty nation. With each passing year, the smoke in the skies would grow thicker until the sun was a ball of blood and the armies could no longer see the drones overhead.

I did not know when it would begin. Perhaps a century, or perhaps a mere decade from now. The Raging 2020s.

The story of an American, Leon Czolgosz. Born 1873 in Michigan to parents who'd recently emigrated from Poland. Lived on a farm and worked in the mines until he was 27, at which time he began to read about the riots and protests, laborers demanding their rights. Disaffected with capitalism, Czolgosz stopped working, grew listless. Left the farm and took off for the big cities, Chicago, Cleveland, Buffalo. Attended anarchist rallies, met Emma Goldman, eventually bought a gun. Read that President William McKinley would be in Buffalo attending the Pan-American Exposition. On September 6, 1901, at a little after four in the afternoon, Czolgosz queued in line to shake hands with the president. Secret Service helped him to the front. They were fooled into thinking Czolgosz had injured his hand, which he'd wrapped in a thick bandage. When McKinley offered his own hand, Czolgosz batted it away. He raised his bandaged hand and fired two shots from the gun hidden in the folds. One of the bullets drilled into McKinley's belly. He died a week later.

At his execution, Czolgosz was quoted as saying, "I killed the president because he was the enemy of the people—the good working people. I am not sorry for my crime."

For years I thought I could shed my brother and achieve the individuality I had so long sought by doing something terrible, historical, infamous. Something that would set us apart, dispel the miasma of Jeremy's sexuality that was asphyxiating my own and grant me the confidence to carry on even if it was only into the afterlife. Assassination was nothing more than a thought. Two asses, a sin, and a nation. The act was not possible in this age. Laughable, really. It had never been about the president. Jeremy was right: it had always been about sex. And so, I turned from the idea of assassination to that of a simpler yet equally terrible act. I turned to my brother, my sister, Jeremy, Jer: Jeri. *Jeralda*. I turned to the Church of the Manifested. I was in the summer of my thirty-sixth year, a true believer in the values that cement Church to States, firmly set on the path against those responsible for the decline of my country.

Patriot.

THE FUTURE MISSIONARY, blond, blue-eyed with a quarterback's build, so obviously American and wearing a dark suit and tie, as if for a funeral, sat behind the podium, between his parents, both of whom held hands, not wanting to let him go just yet. On the other side of the podium sat this outpost's Corporal and his two female attendants. The Torrance outpost's Corporal was a big man. Glasses, short hair thinning into baldness, formidable jowls. When I had walked through the front door of the Torrance CotM outpost that Sunday morning in early July, the Corporal had been there to greet me with a handshake and a welcoming smile. I had accepted both gratefully. "Stan Pangborn, sir," I'd answered to the request for my name.

"Stan. Is this your first time with us?"

"At this outpost, yes. I'm here with Brannigan and Raybury."

The Corporal beamed broadly and patted my shoulder. "Fine young men," he said. "Welcome."

I headed into the main hall where the service was to be held. Already quite a few members were sitting in pews, their posture straight, their gaze determined, concentrated on the dais at the front of the spacious room. Mothers bounced babies in their laps and cautioned their older children to quit horsing around. Only I had come alone.

I spotted Brannigan conversing with a light-eyed mother and her shifting teenage daughter, both of whom were dressed in their Sunday finest. Brannigan turned when he sensed me approaching. His already wide smile grew wider still. "Stan," he said, "Good of you to make it!" We shook hands, and Brannigan introduced me as a Non-Manifested to the two women. Their stares did little to offset my good mood. I looked around the main hall and took in the many families and friends congregating. They chatted, hugged, kissed. Nothing sinister about them, or about any of this. It was only normal, natural, the cure for the greatest disease of all. *This is what it should be like*, I thought. I felt my eyes begin to well up as I watched. The hall lifted with light and energy and words. This was what I wanted. To think: I had been an outcast for so long, and now I was on the cusp of joining what I no longer ridiculed and feared.

Brannigan advised me to take a seat at the back of the room where Raybury was waiting. I left Brannigan with the girl and her mother. Seeing me approach, Raybury drew his legs together. I took a seat beside him and said, "This is really something."

"Sure is."

"All these happy people."

"They're more than happy people, Stan. They're the Manifested. We're truly blessed."

The ceiling stopped high above. The walls were nondescript, much like the outside of the building. No murals, no engravings, no paintings or statues of a crucified Christ either. Instead: a massive screen mounted above the dais. The screen was filled with names, and as I watched, a new name was added every few seconds.

Brannigan joined us just as the service got underway. We watched the Corporal enter and seat himself between his two attendants. The mother, father and their soon-to-be missionary son smiled from where they sat on the other side of the dais. All in the congregation opened their copies of the Book of the Manifested and sang the Mighty Hymns together, as one. My voice was strong, my plan severe and absolute.

With the cessation of our singing came the call for the mother of the future missionary to please approach the podium. She did, teary-eyed and tentative. She greeted those gathered and explained that although she understood how important it was for her son Eli—and The Church and Our Invincible Father—she was nevertheless having a tough time accepting the fact that her 18-year-old would be off proselytizing in Vermont for the next year, starting tomorrow. Watching this woman, I thought of Linda. Would I ever accept Mom the way she accepted Jeremy when he came out at Eli's age? I must, I thought. I must at least put up the front of acceptance at the end of this month when I visited Anomar with Jeri. I would show love for Linda as I should always have. I listened to this Manifested mother as if I were her son. Perhaps I should have been her son, Eli my brother, separate and secure in our sexuality.

"If he can Manifest just one boy," Eli's mother was saying. "Just one guy..." She had a funny story to tell. One night, when Eli was much younger, around six or seven, he was in no mood to take a bath, so he decided to fool her. After sticking his head in the toilet bowl, he emerged from the bathroom, his hair sopping wet, a big smile on his face, and claimed he'd just taken a bath. Honest, Mom, I really did. She wasn't fooled, though she thought the trick cute. "The point is," Eli's mom told those gathered in the outpost main hall, "boys will be boys. We must never forget that truth. It's the ultimate truth in this world. Boys will be boys, and men will be men. They're just going to do what they're going to do, and we must accept whatever that may be. I know Eli will spread this message wide and reach the folks who otherwise wouldn't listen. He's a very capable Man."

Eli's father, whose hair was white and whose hands shook, raised the microphone to his level. "Well, this is the big day," he said. "I kept putting it off. I kept telling myself it's still a long ways off, and now it's here and I'm not sure what to do except say goodbye. Tomorrow my son gets on a plane and flies to Montpelier—that's the capital of Vermont, I found out. I don't even know if I'm pronouncing it right, but I know it's French. It's on the other side of the country, and the thing about Vermont is it's small, and there aren't many people living there, and it's not as diverse as California. I mean they don't have different viewpoints, or they don't allow different viewpoints, I've heard. Very Blue there. Lots of liberals. Eli hopes to change that. We all do. That's what this is about. Changing minds. Manifesting souls. Preparing for The Savior. Eli knows it's going to be tough. He's certainly going to give it his best effort. He's ready, and maybe my wife and I aren't quite ready but we will be. We will be."

The Corporal was nodding, his eyes closed. His attendants, youthful, wide-eyed and bright, held their breath as Eli stood up. The teen pressed his palms against the side of the podium and leaned his mouth into the microphone. His voice uneven with shifting emotions, he told those gathered of how he'd been tempted to engage in political discussions at his high school by teachers and peers and even an administrator. He'd been tempted to think critically about what the other side believed, where they were coming from, and what they felt. Eli was proud to announce that he shut down this temptation at every turn. He kept his mind closed to the other side, the enemy, those False Americans. The Leader did not want that kind of discourse. No True Leader did.

"Sure," Eli said. "I wanted to be friendly with kids at school, I wanted to get good grades and not make trouble with my teachers. It took a lot to deny what they were saying. All that information sounded true, but I knew in my heart it wasn't. Invincible Father helped. The Invincible, Mighty Spirit would enter me in my times of trouble. I would close my eyes in class and feel the Invincible run through me like electricity. The girls around me especially thought I was weird, but I kept telling myself *They're going to see who's in charge in the end.* Some of the guys understood. I wasn't alone. Not everyone was against the Manifested at my school."

The Corporal was now awake and attentive as Eli quoted from a passage in the Book of the Manifested: Conrad chapter 16 verses 2 – 3, the parable of the weak sheep. If a shepherd looks after a hundred sheep and sees that one of them is weak, sickly, not like the others, he doesn't help that sheep. He doesn't waste his time nursing it back to health. He ignores it. He lets it die. He focuses on the sheep he *can* save. And when he strengthens the other 99 sheep he rejoices for *them*, for they are far mightier than the one sheep that was unfortunate enough to stand out as weak or sickly.

"There will come a day," Eli said, "when everyone in this country will think the same, from the very low to the very high, because even the holdouts, the ones who thought differently, couldn't take the feeling of being left out any more and gave in. Someday, I hope someday soon, there will be more of us than there will be of them. And then, one day, there won't be any of them. There will be only us. Because they will *be us* too. Whoever's left will cross that line and join the winning side, because being a loser is just too sad. They'll realize they thought wrong, their beliefs were causing them to be miserable all the time, always worrying about what you don't have to worry about, always angry about some problem that's only in *your* mind. What is there to worry about when you're one of us? What is there to be angry about when you're Manifested? I don't understand all the upset people in this country, in this world, who resist us. I understand they're different, but they don't have to be. That's just it. They don't have to be."

I watched as the Corporal and his two attendants nodded. Indeed, all those that I could see gathered in the great hall nodded, so I did as well.

"I know the Book of the Manifested is true," Eli—soon to be known only by his last name, Douglas—said. "I know The Leader is right in all things, with a direct link to Our Invincible Father in The Invincible Fortress."

I watched Douglas take his seat between his parents, and then I looked to Brannigan and Raybury, then at all those around me, and in their eyes I saw the fullness of my faith restored.

. . .

TWO HOURS LATER, after the Sunday school session had let out, I stood in the long hallway flanked by three Manifested girls: Spencer (cracked but pleasant smile, glasses, rosy face, some acne, tangled hair), Milas (large dark eyebrow, small sweet hands), and Lofton (tall for a girl standing next to Stan Pangborn, all spindly sticks and nervous fingers). These three young women stood close together as if strung through by wire. They nodded at even the things I said that did not warrant a nod. Talking at them, I felt powerful.

Brannigan emerged from the room in which we'd received our lesson. Trailing him were that hopeful mother and her eager-eyed daughter, Lilith. After exchanging a few more pleasantries, they departed and Brannigan joined me and the trio of female Manifested. Congregants passed by on their way out. I smiled and nodded at each of them, even the young children who at one point during the service had gathered up on the dais and sung a song about the arduous 1903 journey from Louisiana to Arizona.

Since he'd set foot inside my apartment, at times I had seen suspicion, even anger in Brannigan's eyes. Now those eyes held only gentleness and affection.

"I think she likes you," I told him.

"Who, Lily? Yeah..."

I punched him on the shoulder. Brannigan took it like a Man. Spencer tittered.

"Her parents are old friends with my folks."

"So you think she'll be your Perfect?"

Grinning, Brannigan looked away. "I don't know," he said. "She's just one girl. I have plenty of others I could work on. I'll keep my options open."

Raybury appeared and offered his hand. "Thanks for coming, Stan. See you tomorrow, six o'clock?"

"That time every day until we're done, if that's possible."

"It's definite," said Brannigan.

For a while I stood in front of the CotM Torrance outpost and remembered. Stan Non-Man, Maddy's nickname for me in Anomar, coined after watching the video they'd shown her in early morning Manifestation class one Tuesday. *What to do if a Non-Man shows interest in you.* Maddy had laughed off that morning's lesson, and I had trusted her disaffection not only with the video but with her religion as well.

On the way back to Hermosa, I cranked up the volume on the classic rock station. I felt good. An achievable goal was in sight. This was more than doable; this was essential. I was not wrong for what I planned. I was only right.

THIS MEMORY I hold onto above all others: Jeremy and I, nine years old, hiking to the Devil's Punchbowl in the low-lying mountains on the outskirts of the San Diego Country Gems. It is early summer and we have disobeyed our parents. We were told to stay inside while they were away at work. But the Pangborn Twins could not remain indoors—not when they had their own work to do. We know the way to the Punchbowl; Frank took us there once with the other Cub Scouts in our den. The walk through the Gems is long but easy; the sun won't ravage us today. Still, we carry a gallon jug of water. Better to be safe. No one knows we're here, and we have not seen anyone else this morning.

The trail, baked and cracked from heat and erosion, descends into a sweeping valley. On either side we see evidence of a great fire. Bushes blackened, trees charred and lying in pieces as if felled by a mighty flaming ax. To us, the valley is prehistoric, vast and stunning in its primordial clarity. Everything around us is sharp, immediate. The earth smells of flesh. We have entered a world in which pterodactyls glide overhead, a stegosaurus forages off in the distance. We imagine we can hear rumblings of a herd on the horizon, and for once we are unafraid.

We reach the Devil's Punchbowl, an icy dark pool filled by a waterfall towering above. The waterfall is gushing fiercely out of the mountainside and into the rocky basin. At the end of summer it's a trickle, the pool nearly empty, but now in mid-June is a different sight. We climb a boulder that juts out over the pool below. The drop doesn't look that far down. We strip to stand naked. No one to see us. No one to scold or shame us. Briefly, a fear passes through, the sum of which is this: Frank and Linda don't know we're here, and what if, after diving into the water, one or both of their sons don't resurface?

We do not have long to fear what might happen, for suddenly the brothers, the Pangborn Twins, have gripped hands and together we are leaping off the boulder, falling with the rush of water pounding in our ears. As we fall, we scream nonsense words, gibberish, tongues. We land smack in the water, and the shock drives up our spines and into our brains. "It's super cold," I shout in between gasps for air and sputterings of water. "Titanic cold!" Jeremy agrees. He waves his hands in the air as if he's drowning—and maybe he is, maybe something has latched onto him below the surface. What might lurk at the bottom of this natural pool, what prehistoric beast is about to drag my brother to the bottom—or simply swallow him whole? I dare not duck my head beneath the surface to gauge the pool's depth. Instead, I concentrate on our accomplishment. "Now we're really baptized!" I say.

We spend an hour sunning ourselves on the rocks around the Punchbowl. We've put our shorts back on by now, and we lounge like lizards, our farmer tans and spaghetti-strand arms still exposed. We don't say anything to each other. We don't need to; our twinship is that strong. At this time, when we are only nine years old, our bond is one of the few things we possess that is truly ours.

When we arrive home, Linda is in the living room. We tell her we went for a walk around the neighborhood, as Frank had often advised we do in the summer when we grew tired of reading or playing video games or watching movies. She doesn't believe us. She notices the dampness of our clothes, the mud and sand on our shoes, the burs in our socks, what we could not have picked up while walking along the paved suburban streets. Linda doesn't demand a confession, and that night Jeremy and I go to bed believing we've been saved.

Seven

I f I could see through walls and into their bedroom, would I be all that surprised? Would I be all that disgusted, all that shocked and outraged? Would I be any more surprised and disgusted, shocked and outraged—and fearful—at the act I myself had failed to fully commit to for my entire existence? Or would I see Jeri and Eric for who they were: two humans in love and showing it.

Here, above the covers so I could see, they fucked openly. Exposure meant nothing to them. Their bodies fit perfectly; they were perfect, and as they moved into one another I felt shame for my posturing and effrontery. I could never show love that real—not toward anyone, not even my father. Instead I hid behind excuse after excuse in the form of systems, organizations, ideas, hate. If I had been confident and secure and safe—

—But you weren't raised to be that way, Stan. Tell them about Frank.

I'd rather not.

—Tell them. Or I will.

You will not. This is *my* book, remember. Now, if you'll excuse me, I have to write this scene between you and Eric.

—You're not required to write it, brother. Certainly not for this book. I don't need your overly earnest, entirely inaccurate descriptions, your awkward recreations of what you assume Eric and I say in bed after we've done it. What you're doing with the Church of the Manifested is offensive enough. You know, I wish you wouldn't call it 'the act.' Sex isn't a stage play we're in. Not something to watch from the side.

Says you.

—You prefer to watch, don't you. Instead of participate. So passive, Stan, and so aggressive. Like you have two minds in that head of yours.

I do, Jer. I do.

—*Jeri*, Stan. Jeri. Please.

I'm sorry. I need to tell them about your career as an MFT and Eric's running UT's site and social media.

—Wait. Are you saying we're *people*, Stan?

That's what I'm saying, yes. And I'd like to—

—Shut it, Stan. I know how this ends.

Don't be that way, Jeri. I know you. You're my br—you're my sister, right? My—

—That's all you know. All you've ever cared to know. And Eric—

I know what Eric did to me, the last day of senior year.

—Oh? He 'did' something to you? Queer minds would like to know.

On that day, the last day of senior year, I found the letter from Maddy in an envelope left under my windshield wiper. It read

stan my silence is fear and i don't know how to control it

i fear for my brother i fear for you
now i know you never liked me like you claimed
it was always hard for me to believe
and anyway what does it matter
my voice is like a guy's it's so deep
i'll never be anyone's perfect
it was never going to be you anyway
even if you weren't
my church has always kept any nonmanifested away
nonmans aren't supposed to pursue manifested
i want to welcome you into our family but it's so dangerous
my parents
now i understand why you put on an act around me
it's like you're two people really
i know why you do this stan
it tears me apart to see you do this
it hurts
soon you won't have to
you won't have to prove anything to anyone
in college i hope you'll have the confidence to show everyone
who you really are

Maddy's house wasn't far from the high school. I pulled into the dirt roundabout, the large oak tree in the center, and got out. Maddy was sitting on the front porch.

I held up the letter. "I don't understand," I said.

"Stan," she said. "I know. I know about—"

"Your brother and my brother, I know."

"What?" she said.

I backed away. I had suspected for a while now, but hearing myself speak the truth clarified all those years of confusion leading up to this moment and solidified my previously suppressed rage. I turned and ran. Maddy might have called out to me—some question about the existence of my brother.

Rather than return to my car, I ran around the side of the Donaldson house. Jeremy must be here, with Eric. The shed was dark and wide as a mouth. Afternoon sunlight filtered in through the one window. I entered to find Eric kneeling on the ground, finishing up a large canvas that showed the figure of a man from the waist up, covered in shiny scales. Eric saw me and stood, smiling, his hands sweeping the sides of his cargo pants. He'd grown thinner and taller and had let his light brown hair grow out over his ears. He had Maddy's eyes. "Hey," he said, and before I could recoil he rushed up and wrapped his arms around me. I did not turn my face when his lips brushed mine. An electric, familiar feeling. I pushed him away.

"I am not my brother!" I said.

"Brother?" Eric said. "Stan, what are you—"

—Don't stop, Stan. Keep going.

That's all they need to know.

—You've been in denial—

Fuck you, Jeri. I didn't do anything. He did it to me.

—Eric helped me discover who I am. That summer before our senior year Stan and I would go over to the Donaldson house, and it was hot in that shed and Stan never entered, he was trying with Madeline so much, and Eric and I talked about how my brother needed a girl a lot more than I needed someone, I wasn't sure it had to be a girl, and so Eric and I got to talking about how it was between Stan and Madeline, how she should have just taken my brother to the Anomar outpost one night, found a room, locked the door, and stripped him where he stood. Place her hands all over him, under him. To do it in the Church of the Manifested—not for him but for herself. To have all the power over a guy, a Non-Man. As the ultimate fuck you to CotM. But even Eric agreed his sister would never do it. And it was like Stan was trying to squeeze his pinhead through a pinhole, he was so dead-set to do right by this girl. Stan Non-Man. And when I at last understood what I felt for Eric, for men not women, I went to him and he took me, took me as no man, not even our father, had held me in his arms. God, I wish this were my book.

I make no apologies, Jeri. I am what I am. This is what it is.

—And what it is is a mask you've worn all our lives. Tell them what you did next.

I got back in the car, turned on the radio, and sped away. Elton John's "Levon" was on the radio. I foresaw the Second Civil War.

HE PICKED up on the fourth buzz.

"Stan," he said.

"Jeri," I said.

"Thanks. And if you could use 'they' and 'them' for my pronouns. For now. You can stop with the 'he-she,' 'brother-sister' combo talk."

"Fine. So, Maddy called. I'm coming."

"Don't fuck with me, Stan."

"I'm not. Honest. I'll be there, a little over a month from now."

"I find that impossible to believe."

"Believe me. Please. I want to make it up to you."

Silence as my brother waited. At last, they said, "You'll have to explain yourself."

"It's not right, what I've been thinking all our life. I want to attend your wedding because I want to show I've accepted you. And Eric. I'm over it."

"You've accepted me. Accepted us." Jeri laughed as if I'd said the funniest thing they'd ever heard. I was hurt. My words sounded convincing enough to me.

"What?"

"Excuse me if I still don't believe you, brother. Forget the fact that we haven't said this many words to each other in I don't know how many years. If that's the truth then I'm not *feeling* it from you now."

"Jeri. Can you forgive me? I want you to please forgive me."

"Right now? Just like that."

"You can take a day. Or two. You can wait till we're in Anomar together at the end of this month."

"We're not going to be together in Anomar at the end of this month."

"That's what I wanted to offer: a chance for us to spend time together before you get hitched. I was hoping you'd hang out with me, face-to-face, just you and me."

"And Mom."

"And Linda. Right."

"The Pangborn Twins ride again."

"Will you?"

"I'll think about it."

"I am sorry."

"You're sorry."

"I am. I—I take responsibility. I haven't been a brother to

you for so long. All our life, really. I was never good to you. Do you remember? The things I did to you.... Do you?"

—Of course I do.

"Of course I do."

"I'm sorry for all those things. I really am. I need you to forgive me. Please."

"You? Stan Pangborn, my brother.... *You* want to be forgiven for your transphobia, your homophobia, your misogyny, your bigotry and your opportunistic, narcissistic personality, all the teasing and taunting and bullying and belittling and physical, mental and emotional shit you put me through when we were young."

"I do. I do."

"It's like forgiving the devil himself, Stan."

"Please."

When next Jeri spoke, their voice was thick and tremulous. "You want me to forgive you? Okay. I forgive you. I forgive my brother, Stan Pangborn."

"Will you see me? In Anomar?"

"Yes."

"Thank you." Were the tears at the edges of my eyes real? Were theirs?

Rather than cry, we arranged to meet at San Diego International Airport then drive to Anomar to see Linda. After a few days spent in our hometown, Jeri would fly back to Austin and I would drive back to Los Angeles. Three weeks later, I would arrive in the Texas capital for their wedding.

During the next four workdays—Thursday, July 9th, Friday July 10th, Monday, July 13th, and Tuesday, July

14th—I spent hours reading the Book of the Manifested. I called in sick. Turned off my phone. Shut myself away from Simone and the few others I knew in my life.

I was alone and I was among friends.

Proof was in the text.

Men may one day live as gods. Conrad 17:3. *I have said, Ye will be gods, for all of you now are godlike, imbued even in this common world with immense and magnificent powers.* Conrad 23:1. *And if men, then heirs; heirs of the Invincible One, and joint-heirs of His Kingdom, the Fortress on High. We men suffer with Him so that we may be glorified together.* Conrad 44:8 – 10. *Men, now we are the sons of the Invincible Father, and it doth not yet appear that we shall be rulers: but we know that, when women buckle, we shall be Manifested, and those we control shall be Manifested under us. All men shall be like Him, for we shall see Him as He is and know how a Man must be.* What I read frightened me, for it could be believed if I so desired such power, comfort, escape.

During each of those four days, Brannigan and Raybury visited my apartment. We held the third Manly Talk Monday afternoon, the fourth Tuesday, the fifth Wednesday, the sixth Thursday, and the seventh and final on Friday, July 17th, three days before I was to drive down to San Diego and pick Jeri up. During the talks I learned that all religions except the Church of the Manifested were false. In these first two decades of the 21st century, all other religions were struggling with declining membership. They had lost their way, the numbers the greatest proof. Not so with CotM, whose numbers were skyrocketing. CotM, the one true religion, is spreading Invincible Father's message far and wide. In recent years, The Church has pulled back on overseas proselytizing and chosen instead to focus on converting those living in the United States. The coming war, Raybury mentioned.

"There's going to be a war?"

"A war for control of this country," Brannigan said. "The Church is preparing for it."

No unclean thing can dwell in the presence of The Invincible.

"When I die," I said, "and I get everything I've ever desired, will I get to choose who joins me in The Invincible Fortress—and who doesn't?"

"Our Invincible Father will have a say," Brannigan said, "but if you have a good reason for not wanting someone to join you, your wish should be granted."

"When Jeri dies, they'll have a chance to go to The Invincible Fortress?"

"There's a chance. In your...in their case, it would be a slim chance."

"Long odds," I said.

"We won't turn anyone away," said Raybury, "but if we're going to be honest here, there's some we'd prefer not to have."

Outside of the talks, I kept odd hours, avoided my phone and the knocks at my door. The number one worst sin—worse even than murder: *Thou shalt not settle for anyone or anything.* At night, at a time when I'd always been asleep, I stayed up and recited verses aloud, my voice strong, my self secure. *Nevertheless the man can be without the woman and find another, but the woman can never be without the man, in The Invincible.* I thought of Simone and Maddy, the Pangborns, CenterPost in Phoenix, the end. Now we're baptized.

Finally, after falling asleep, I would encounter dreams, nightmares, future flashes of the Second Civil War. These premonitions intensified during those mid-July days. Strip by strip, I was tearing away from the old and adhering to the new.

"How's the reading coming along, Stan?"

"Excellent. I'm just over three-quarters of the way through. I read close to a hundred pages last night."

"A hundred pages *in one night*?"

"Do you want me to quote something? I can quote anything now, on the spot."

Raybury uttered a *hooyah* quietly, respectfully.

"That bodes well, Stan," said Brannigan. "You're showing yourself to be a true Man."

"We won't have to shoot you," Raybury said.

"What?"

"Tell him the joke, Raybury."

"Okay, here's the joke. This pair of missionaries has spent all this time on this one guy. Pretty young guy, not much older than them. They're on the last of the Manly Talks, and that's when it comes out that the guy hasn't been doing any of the reading, nothing, he's just been faking his interest the whole time. Just to mess with them. Mess with The Church. Now he wants them out. He thinks they'll just leave. He thinks we're weak. Oh, we'll go, the missionaries say, but first we have do the Wrap Up. What's the Wrap Up? the guy asks. Is that like a final prayer? Yeah, something like that, the missionaries say, and then they take out their guns and shoot him right in the chest, dead."

Raybury brayed and Brannigan guffawed, so I gave a chuckle.

"Quite a joke, huh?"

"I'll say. What did they do with the body?"

"Oh they just left it there, on the couch, as a warning."

"I see. Uh, do you guys carry?"

"Well, Stan," Brannigan said, dead-serious now, "you're on our side, so you won't have to find out."

Raybury barked out another *hooyah*, this one far more forceful.

It was the first time I'd answered my phone in well over a week.

"Stan," she said.

"Simone. Hi."

"You don't sound concerned."

"Concerned about what?"

"Oh, you know, *your job*. Theresa wanted me to tell you Walter is about ready to blow. Just because you're a manager doesn't make you immune."

"I've been at work."

"No, you haven't, Stan. You've been an extender for a week now. Are you dying?"

"A part of me is. The old part."

Simone sighed. "The only reason I bothered to call is that I have to. Now I have to care about you."

I was unaware of what she was insinuating. When she did come out with it, I was saying, "I care about you too. That's why—"

"Stan. I'm pregnant."

At the dreaded p-word my entire body turned in on itself in a rattled compression. I had trouble breathing, yet I felt ready to vomit.

"I'm pregnant," Simone repeated.

"No," I managed to eke out.

"You try being in my body, Stan. You try being sick every morning for the past week. When I took a pregnancy test and it came out—"

"It's not true," I said.

"You are so fucking *narrow*. I will take you to the doctor, to court, to wherever to convince you."

"Oh God. Simone. I'll—I'll pay for the abortion."

"What?"

Her question as written down here does not do justice to the outrage I heard from her then. I realized my mistake.

"I just thought…"

"You *thought*?" she seethed. "You thought you'd just kill this child? You thought I'd kill it with you? You've always been a presumptuous prick, Stan Pangborn. You assumed—"

I, I am sinless, and the root of sin derives from me.

"Simone, please."

I am lust in (outward) appearance—

—and interior self-control exists within me.

"How—"

"You fucked me—that's how!"

"But you're on the pill."

"You *assumed* I was on the pill, Stan. That I wasn't taking a break from it for other reasons."

"You lied to me, you—"

"You wouldn't let me *speak*! You got me to the point where I was *scared* to bring it up with you because I didn't know what you were capable of doing to me. You are some kind of demon, Stan Pangborn. A monster—"

"I am every other man in this world, every single guy out there is me, hidden or not."

"Then this world sucks," said Simone.

"The pool," I said. "You told me the chlorine in your parents' pool that afternoon would keep it from happening. I shouldn't have trusted you."

"Yeah, sure, maybe that was the moment," Simone said facetiously. "Or maybe it was when the condom didn't hold because you just couldn't accept it on you."

Abstinence, I thought. Celibate.

"At least I got one real fuck out of you," Simone said.

"Real," I scoffed.

"Plenty of couples fuck in swimming pools, Stan. *That's* normal."

"Simone. Listen to me. It was a mistake. We need to start over."

"We're not starting over, Stan. We're having this child. Or at least I am."

"I want you to be with me this weekend. Sunday is very important."

"Stan—do you hear yourself?"

"I'm going to another Invincible Meeting in Torrance."

"This is your child as much as mine."

"You're my Perfect, Simone. I know that now. I believe that. We need to go together to the outpost and show a united front to the Corporal. As a co—"

"Fuck you!" she screamed. "When I have this child and she gets to a certain age, I'm going to tell her that her father wanted to kill her when she wasn't even out of my body yet. That's the kind of evil demon you are..."

"We need to go. For us. The Church will save us. It's

already made me so much better. I have to leave for San Diego the day after the service, but Brannigan and Raybury would be willing to talk to—"

I stopped as I realized I'd been speaking to an empty dial tone.

"*YOU'RE* the guy who runs the *From Adam* site? *You're* Adam?"

"You got me. Guilty as charged. I'm surprised you read it."

"We've been reading it for a while," Raybury said. "Since we were in high school. Isn't that right, Brannigan?"

The older missionary nodded. "Why does it surprise you?"

"Oh," I said. "It's just...you being religious and all."

"I hope it's clear by now, Stan," Brannigan said, "that we're not really even a religion at this point. We're a force."

"A force to be reckoned with," said Raybury.

Brannigan said, "You're lucky, Stan. We feel comfortable with you. We can't say that about every guy we meet. You're wise to what's going on. You've been in on the whole thing for a while now."

"Yes. I admire so much..."

"We know."

"You write the truth, Stan," said Brannigan. "Now we need you to act on that truth—for yourself and for this country."

"INVINCIBLE FATHER'S MARRIED, right? What about Invincible Mother?"

"She's not invincible, Stan. We don't use that word when we speak of her. Or any girl."

"She fails," Raybury said. "All the time."

"Even in The Invincible Fortress?"

"She's not actually in The Invincible Fortress. At least not permanently. No woman really lives there. Only when Invincible Father allows her in, then she can be there with Him, until He says that's enough and sends her out."

"She's just on the outside," said Brannigan.

"All the women are," I affirmed.

"And He chooses who He wants, when He wants."

"And I can do the same?"

"We all can," Brannigan said, "as long as you're with us and not against us."

"Do you think there'll be a woman president?"

"Here? In America?"

"No," Brannigan said. "That's impossible. Look who's running in next year's election."

"They say she has a good chance."

"Never," reiterated Brannigan. "Even when we're old and gray and in nursing homes, we'll still have a man in the White House."

"We may even have a Man in the White House someday." Raybury grinned.

"It always has to be a man," I said.

"Even women don't want a woman president. The thought of it makes too many of them uncomfortable."

"They've been trained," Raybury said.

"I want to believe you're right."

"Believe, Stan. Everyone's saying she's going to win, but they don't understand this country. We do."

I smiled, nodded, and remembered those words, now false, I'd written in a letter to Madeline Donaldson the summer before we entered college: *I'm not perfect though I tried for so long we both did Maddy that's the truth there's nothing more the strength lies within me now and not from others or from him that's my religion it's called Individualism you should try it Madeline it's where you rely on your own values and strengths as a decent human being you don't rely on a god or a priest or a doctrine or the possibility of heaven or hell rely on no one but yourself and you will be content this doesn't mean be reclusive and shun people only look long and hard at yourself and accept yourself for who you are and know you're special in your own eyes and the eyes of others.*

What others? I now wondered while laughing along with the Manifested.

You *can* be perfect.

EIGHT

Our waiter, a middle-aged man wearing glasses and a garish Hawaiian shirt, stood impatiently with pen poised over pad, ready to write. His skin was weathered, and his long black hair had been braided into a whip that fell behind his back.

Frank asked if I wanted utensils.

"No, I'm fine, Dad. Sticking with these." I held up my pair of chopsticks.

Frank smiled at the waiter and asked for two sets of utensils. The waiter's demeanor soured. His brow furrowed and he stared hard at the notepad, the pen hovering, as if he wanted to write anything down other than my father's request. He tapped his pen twice on the pad and put both items away. What little was left of his forced smile vanished. "I'll be out with those," he said brusquely before hurrying off.

Frank watched him leave, then faced me. His demeanor too had soured.

"I didn't want to get into it with you," he said, "but if you'd just asked for the utensils too we would have all been together on this, united, and he wouldn't have any cause to compare you to us."

"Frank," my father's girlfriend, Taun, who looked like a man, warned.

"I'm sorry," I said. "I can still ask—"

"No. It's too late," Frank said, and he sat back and would not look at me. His heavy hand shot out, gripped his bottle and slammed the beer back. He glugged. I watched him, flashes of memory like a strobe light. "I shouldn't even have to ask for a fork and knife here," he said. "Last time I checked, we're in Santa Barbara, not Tokyo."

He checked his phone, so I did too.

"He's having a bad night," said Taun. I avoided looking at her. Him? (Them?) My father's girlfriend had to be a woman. Short hair, but many women sported that style. A masculine shape to the facial structure, the jaw, but the voice was feminine enough. My father would not have—

—The truth, Stan. That's all we ask of you.

"Remember that time, honey," Taun continued, her hand on my father's arm, "when we were in Bangkok at that really great restaurant. I say great only because of the food."

"The food was spectacular," Frank grunted.

"And there were all these people rushing around, and it took us a while to figure out they were customers, and we had to play the role of the waiters! We had to go in back, it was just this huge commune, and wrangle up our food from the cooks."

"A memorable experience," Frank said.

"So many memorable experiences with you, honey."

They held hands. I forced myself to look. The hair on Taun's forearms, the hairs on the back of her fingers. She was transforming before my eyes—transitioning from the woman I had assumed she would be to the truth of what my father had always wanted.

"Retirement's been good to you," I said.

My father, 29 years my senior, nodded. He and Taun were headed to Tokyo in two days.

I asked if either of them had heard of seppuku.

"Of course," Taun said. "When you take your sword and slice yourself down the middle. Like in that movie with Tom Cruise. The Japanese one."

"*The Last Samurai*," my father said.

"Yes, that's the one. What a great movie."

"It was all right," said Frank. "I didn't like the ending. I'll take him in any *Mission Impossible* any day over the bleeding heart stuff."

"What bleeding heart stuff?"

"The bleeding heart stuff at the end. That stuff never sits well with me."

My father and his woman noticed me holding up one of my chopsticks. Frank asked what I was doing.

"You have to think," I said, "with seppuku, it's so gruesome." As I spoke I demonstrated with my one chopstick. "You open yourself up, gut yourself like a fish, and your 'second' who's standing behind you lops off your head. I wonder if that's why the Japanese eat with chopsticks. They can't be used as weapons. Eating's supposed to be a peaceful act."

"We may find out the truth," Frank said. "I'll send it in a postcard."

"Thanks," I said. "I appreciate the postcards, all of them. I was really surprised when you DM'd me."

"We were in town," Frank said. "I wanted to see my son."

He looked me over for another time that evening. I could feel his eyes boring into me like twin drills. I shifted in my seat. "You're doing well for yourself," he said. "Successful. Do you have a girlfriend?"

"Yes," I lied.

"Pictures?"

I showed my father a few photos of Simone on my phone.

"No, son. Not those kind of pictures. The other ones. The dirty ones—"

"Frank!" Taun swatted my father playfully. "Let the boy be, why don't you."

"I would hope he's not a boy anymore. He's 36, right? That shouldn't be a boy. That's gotta be a man by now." My father stared me down. "You'd call yourself a man by now, right, Stan?"

I had trouble getting the piece of steak down my throat just then. It caught. I gulped and cleared the obstruction, but my eyes watered, and my face reddened with embarrassment. Our waiter returned just then with the utensil sets, which he handed over to Taun and then retreated—this time without inquiring if anyone would like anything else.

"I need another beer," said Frank.

"That's probably enough, honey."

"We're taking a cab, aren't we?" To me, my father said, "I saw you almost choke just now. Not a good way to die, son. Ask for a knife already."

A man uses a knife. An American uses a knife.

"I will," I said, my eyes on my plate. "The next time he comes around."

"If he ever does come back. It's his problem anyway." My

father offered me his knife, blade first. "Stay alive," he said. "You're all I have left."

"I'm hungry, Dad. A man doesn't wait, right? A man's gotta eat."

Frank and Taun again united hands above the table, their fingers speaking. I tried to ignore their display of affection. I swallowed another piece of steak. "See?" I said. "These pieces are small. I'm fine."

I'm strong, Dad. Really. Like you.

"Steak is the number one food people choke to death on," Frank stated.

"I know the Heimlich, honey," Taun said. They patted my father's forearm.

My father said, "I for one would hate to choke to death in front of anyone."

"Well it won't happen tonight, okay?" I picked at the breathy rice, the tempura, shrimp and fish. I stabbed a piece of chicken and brought it to my mouth, taking half the piece away with my teeth. I gnashed and tried not to look at my father. I had been looking at him all my life. I had always seen him as grander, mightier than life, certainly grander, mightier than me. He had taken up all my space, all my thinking for so long. Tonight was no different. But I tried. Instead of him I observed the high-backed red leather booth we sat in, the low-hanging globe that threw soft light onto the table's surface, where I caught a faint reflection. "And even if it did happen," I said, because I couldn't stop or help myself, "and Taun here couldn't save me with the Heimlich, so what? The afterlife awaits."

"There is no afterlife, son."

"You used to believe there is."

"Not anymore."

"But there is an afterlife," I said. "*My* kind of afterlife, where *I* control everything—and everyone."

"That's scary," said Taun.

"Dad, I know you think this way. I know you fear losing control of everything too."

Frank nodded, uttered a word that might have been *Yes* under his breath.

I said, "We are control freaks, you and I. What happens when we've lost all control and we're at the mercy of some other power, not our own? What happens then?"

"You've gained some real insight into life, I see."

"I have. I've grown up."

"You're not the little snot-nosed kid in my house anymore," my father said. I'd like to think the look he gave me was one of appreciation, but I couldn't be certain.

"God is merciful," Taun said.

"No he's not. He's Moloch, destroyer of children. He devours those placed on the altar by their parents, the parents dissatisfied with what they've raised. Dad, you used to read to me Leviticus 18, 20, you know what I'm talking about. You agree! That's my god: Moloch."

"You've changed," Frank said. Was that some small degree of fear I saw in his eyes? Did I at last have control?

"I've always been the way I am now," I countered. "The only difference is that now I've found a way through my brother, and myself."

"Still talking crazy," Frank told Taun. "I guess that hasn't changed."

"Until the day I die," I said. "I'm so happy now...I know

now my funeral is going to be packed. Anyone who doesn't show up is going to miss out."

"Why is that, son?"

"There's going to be a ton of people, and music, Van Morrison, Talking Heads, it'll be a rock concert to blow all other funerals away."

Taun stared at me as if they were looking at a great work of art smeared with blood.

I smiled. "The Church of the Manifested has shown me the way through," I announced.

"The Church of the Manifested, huh." Frank asked his partner what they wanted their funeral to be like.

"My funeral?"

"Sure. Shoot."

"Just bury me in a pine box out in the woods somewhere."

"The strong woman has spoken," my father said.

Strongwoman.

"You of course know what would be playing at my funeral," Frank said. "'Ring of Fire.'" He belted out a few lines of Cash's hit in a deep bellow.

I laughed because I had to, my eyes squinting shut, and jammed the pair of chopsticks in the half-filled bowl of rice. The chopsticks remained standing up.

"Don't laugh. I expect you to be up there singing it, son."

"If you die first, I will."

I was aware then of a presence on my right. I looked up in time to see our waiter reach over and yank my chopsticks out of the rice bowl. He clenched them in his fist.

"Do you see this," he said, incensed. "Do you know what you did? Don't *ever* do this again! Putting your chopsticks such as this anywhere on the table is a terrible insult."

There followed a brief tableau in which our waiter, Frank, Taun and I stared at the bowl of rice. No one spoke. All the restaurant had hushed.

It dawned on me then that I had offended not just our waiter and the restaurant establishment but the entire Japanese culture as well. "Oh jeez," I said. "Um..."

My father came to my defense. "Look," he said, "I guess what he did wasn't politically correct. I get that. But could you take it down a notch on the anger there?"

"I'd appreciate it," I said, confident now. On this admonishment, my father and I were united.

Inwardly, our waiter raged. "You...you..."

"I didn't mean anything by it," I said. "A simple mistake, right? I can make a mistake. By Invincible Father..."

"*Invincible Father*?" The waiter hung over me like a gallows.

"Yeah. What about Him?"

"Are you CotM?"

"*Hooyah*. I finished the last Manly Talk yesterday."

Our waiter's mouth twisted into a grin. At first, I didn't trust his change in mood. But he spoke: "It's all good," he said. "My sincere apologies for my explosion. I understand you couldn't help yourself. Good luck." Our waiter laid his hand on my shoulder. "May Our Invincible Father be with you."

With that, he smiled and backed away.

After the waiter had left our table, my father turned to me. "That was out of a mafia movie. What's CotM?"

"Church of the Manifested," Taun said.

"You know it?"

"I know about it. I'll tell you more when we're alone." Taun lasered me a chilling look.

I asked Frank if he'd ever heard of Spinoza.

"Who?"

"I have," Taun said. Their eyes still wouldn't leave me be.

"Spinoza," I said, "has this question about worms. When you cut a worm in two, both halves regenerate so you have two whole worms, completely intact. But Spinoza wonders where the soul of the original worm goes. Which regenerated half gets the soul?"

"Is this about that 'brother' of yours?"

"Why do you say it like that?"

—You know why.

"You know why, son." Frank scrunched his mouth up and breathed through his nose.

"Dad. *What do you think*? About *Spinoza*?"

"About the worms? Worms don't have souls." After some silence, Frank added, "Thirty-six years and still overthinking. Still hiding his true self. Still lapping up whatever scraps he can get."

"Frank…"

"But I love you, son. If I didn't I wouldn't be in front of you now. I love you. You're my only child. There's never been any other. I wish you'd just man up already and admit you're angry I left—left you, left your mother. Admitting the anger you have toward me would go a long way to finally making you a man."

"I am going to be a Man," I said. "I don't hate you. I hold no anger toward you."

"That's the problem," my father said. "That's always been your problem. This self-directed…thinking something's there that's never been there." He paused. "You're on your own, you know. You've been on your own your entire life."

.   .   .

RATHER THAN DRIVE back to L.A. that night after dinner, I chose to accept my father's offer of an adjoining room at the hotel where he and his partner were staying.

I checked the nightstand clock when I heard the voices that woke me up. Not shouting, but loud enough to hear through the door separating our rooms. 2:21 AM.

I got out of bed, crept toward the door, and placed my ear against the thin material. I heard

"It's not working itself out."

"I know you can do better. We can always do better."

There's always somebody better.

"The pressure's pointless. It won't work itself out, and it's not going to end. I know myself too well now to be prideful any longer. Such a mistake I made..."

"You can admit it..."

"I can't. How would he see me? How would I see me? That's the worst."

I am a coward and I am the victor.

"He's back in my life. I'm sorry, but I have to go to him. I have to go and tell him what I felt for him then, in college."

"Go. Just come back. You know when the flight leaves."

"I am sorry."

"Don't be. When you fight, you fight with your palms pressed to the ceiling. I don't blame you or him. I don't."

I stood back from the door, debating whether I should open it. After some time, I decided against committing such a rash action. Not wanting to hear the truth any longer, I went to the bathroom, did some business, then returned to bed. When next I awoke it was 4:34 AM. The television threw its savage glow across my bed. On the couch lay my father, Franklin Pangborn. From my vantage point, I could not see his face. I sat up. "Dad," I said. He did not stir. "Dad," I repeated, this time louder. Still no movement.

A fear passed through me that perhaps Frank had died, but when I crawled over the bed and found a good angle, I saw that he was only asleep, breathing quietly in the flickering and the darkness.

NINE

We did not leave the airport until the approach of sundown. From San Diego International we took the 5 south to the 163 north, then switched over to the 15 north before cutting east along highway 67 headed inland. As I drove, I pointed out the features of my new truck. To my surprise, Jeri stayed off their phone and matched my enthusiasm. If they were faking that enthusiasm, they were doing a fine job of it.

We broke free of the winding pass and sighted Anomar as darkness nestled into the valley. In the mornings, in the spring, the great grassy fields on either side would glisten with dew. Spotted with cattle, these now yellow-dry fields suffered under the heat that was at last retiring for the day. In our wake we left the lone farm house I'd always believed was haunted, the long row of mailboxes leaning to our left, across from the sign welcoming visitors to our little town.

Rather than turn right on Elders Road—the quickest way to reach our secluded suburban enclave in the hills, the San

Diego Country Gems—I remained on what was now Main Street. Jeri asked what was up.

"I'm hungry."

"What about Mom?"

"Linda can wait. She's been waiting for years. What's another hour going to matter to her."

Jeri switched stations. In the monotony of changing channels, we heard a voice I recognized. I told them to hold on, stop. As soon as Jeri's hand had left the dial, I reached over and turned up the volume.

"...honor me...and you whisper against me. You honor me...and you whisper against me. You honor me...and you whisper against me. You honor..."

The voice belonged to Father Melvin, the priest who had often come to mass at Mother of Mercy in Anomar drunk when we were kids and one Sunday preached a sermon singling out professional baseball players as the root of society's evils. Father Melvin urged the congregation to take high-powered rifles, affixed with scopes, go to the top of the stands, and as the players charged the field pick them off, as many as we could.

"You honor me...and you whisper against me," I repeated.

"...and now that he's announced his run, we're going to throw our full support behind him, everything we have. He is the Chosen One, my friends..."

Jeri reached for the dial, but I grabbed their forearm and held steady.

"Garbage, Stan, and you know it."

"Just words, Jeri."

"You traffic in this same horseshit. You profit from it, just like Melvin. Politics and religion: the beast with two backs."

I pulled into the Denny's parking lot. We had our choice of seating that Monday night. We slid into a booth and the waitress, who looked the same age as Linda, came by to take our order. Jeri would not look at me after she'd left. They took a sip of water, swished it around in their mouth and swallowed.

"Austin still weird?" I asked.

"I thought you'd never ask. Of course. As weird as ever. The bats are waiting for you. August is their month."

"I can't wait."

"So, when do you convert?"

"I'm not sure I will," I said.

"Such a lie, Stan. I see straight through you."

—For what is inside of you is what is outside of you, and the one who fashions you on the outside is the one who shaped the inside of you.

And what you see outside of you, you see inside of you; it is visible and it is your garment.

I pressed the tines of my fork into the table.

The weapon is us, I thought.

"I'll be back," I said.

I flushed the toilet and opened the stall door to find I was no longer alone. An old man, impeccably dressed in a light suit and dark tie, stood before me. The man was taller than the Pangborn Twins, perhaps six-three or six-four. His eyes were yellow and watery, his skin like canyons. His shoulders hunched forward like the wings of a pterodactyl. He tried to keep his hands clasped together and still he couldn't, they shook too much. I watched them shake. Then I looked up and that's when the old man asked in a voice that shook along with his hands if I wouldn't mind helping him out. I asked him what he meant. With one dangerously unsteady hand, the old man indicated his zipper, and I just about fled the restroom then. Only, I stayed. I stayed because that man looked at me with such pleading eyes, his heart in his throat, I couldn't help picturing him alone in his house or in his apartment or a rest home for all I knew. Alone is what mattered, for isn't loneliness the greatest disease of all?

That's what did it: the idea that this man, whose daily existence consisted of the television and the occasional telemarketer, had dressed to the nines and ventured out, and it was a Monday night, maybe his children had left him, maybe his friends were all dead, his partner dead, maybe no one wanted to talk to him anymore and all he wanted was a little help with the act he struggled to perform every day. It's not like Jeri, I reasoned. It's a sign is what it is. Come on, Stan. Loneliness is a disease greater than love.

So because the old man was human and I, ultimately, am human too, I helped him over to the urinal. Not once did his hands cease shaking. I felt foolish standing there beside him, hesitant to unzip his fly, but I could not cut and run now and so I undid the front of the old man's slacks and watched as his sizable penis flopped out. I thought of Jeri and I thought of Frank. I even thought, however briefly, of Brannigan and Raybury and the Corporal and The Leader. They were all a part of me, and now this elderly gentleman was as well. Okay, how best to do this. Just take it, Stan. He's waiting.

I held the man's penis while he urinated. He didn't take long. "Thank you," he said. "That'll do me, son."

I left him alone in the bathroom and returned to the table. Food had arrived and Jeri was digging in. They kept their eyes on the plate as I slid into the booth. Then, after they had put away a sufficient portion of their meal, Jeri said, "I hope what you're about to do brings you peace, Stan. I hope it finally proves you're straight."

"That's not it."

"That's exactly it, brother. Joining the Church of the Manifested is *exactly* the proof you've been seeking. I mean come on, what better way is there for you? Even though you know there are queer Manifested out in the open about their sexuality."

"No trans, though."

"That's where you draw the line."

"That's where *this country* draws the line."

"History, Stan."

"The future, Jeri."

"The devil you know," they mumbled, loud enough for me to hear. "I don't get it. When does 'I believe' become 'I know'?" They considered. Then: "Say you love me."

"Not here."

"Just once. Say it and mean it."

"We're in the Anomar Denny's, for Invincible Father's sake."

"You've never said it. Not once in all our 36 years. Say it now. Say 'I love you, Jeri.'"

"'I love you, Jeri.'"

They leaned back, their eyes fierce with awareness. They said, "Love the sinner, hate the sin, right?"

"That's right," I said. "I don't hate *you*. It's—"

Jeri shushed me. They pressed in. Our eyes locked. "But don't you see, brother?" they said. "The sinner *is* the sin. The sin is the sinner. You can't separate the two."

I let my fork clatter. "I'm done," I announced. "Let's go see Linda."

THE DOOR to the master bedroom was closed when we entered the house. Jeri turned on the living room lights then took a seat on the couch and untied their shoes. I remained in the tiled entryway.

"What," they said when they saw I still hadn't moved. "You expected she'd be waiting up for us? Come on, brother—"

"We're midway through the second decade of the 21st century," I finished.

"You wouldn't think it, though," Jeri told the carpet.

The door to the master bedroom opened and Linda Pangborn shuffled out. Her face was puffy with newly thrown off sleep, and she looked to be naked beneath her bathrobe. She didn't bother to rub her half-lidded eyes but instead stepped drunk-like and smiling toward me. I greeted her with a generous hug and a kiss on the cheek. Jeri watched from the side.

"Stan," she said. "Welcome home."

"Sorry to wake you, Mom. We tried to be quiet."

"Ah, *we*." She nodded wisely. "Still on that, are you."

I relented and joined Linda and Jeri in the living room. Once the Pangborn Twins were seated Linda asked if I'd like anything to eat or drink. I begged off, explaining that we'd already eaten and would be going to bed soon. Content, Linda nodded. We were kids again ready for our bedtime story. Linda settled into the recliner next to the couch and engaged us in conversation. The flight from Austin to San Diego, the drive from L.A. to San Diego, from San Diego to Anomar. Linda's recent retirement. I could not concentrate, for the door to the master bedroom hung slightly ajar, and although the inside of that room was dark I sensed someone was inside.

The snores issuing from the room were unmistakable now, and fearing that the sound would only grow stronger I rose from the couch just as Jeri said good night to Linda. I swung around the couch and stepped swiftly toward the door.

"Stan," they said sharply.

A fingernail of light from the living room stabbed the bed. On it I saw a man shorter than Frank lying on his stomach wrapped in a sheet. The strength of his snoring only increased as I pushed the door open and stepped into what had been Frank's room. As I drew closer, the man snorted, sniffled and awoke to face Stan Pangborn standing over him.

"You're younger than Mom," I said quietly.

The man mumbled something unintelligible. His hair was just beginning to gray.

"I don't want to know your name," I said. "I only want to know, are you naked? Are you? Are you naked? Are you naked?"

I must have asked the question several more times before the man turned on his side and yanked the sheet over his head. From beneath the sheet, I heard him say, "Now I know who she was talking about."

Jeri and Linda were with me now. I pushed past them both and headed to my old room. "I'm proud of you," I told Linda on my way out.

· · ·

THE NIGHT before our hike to the Devil's Punchbowl, Linda cooked up salmon topped with pesto, fingerling potatoes and asparagus. She served with aplomb. The three of us ate in silence for a good portion of the meal until Jeri said, "Tell her, Stan."

"Tell her what?"

Linda looked at me sadly.

"If you don't, I will."

I did not look at Jeri for fear of revealing my anger.

"All right," I said at last. "Big news. I'm joining the Church of the Manifested."

Linda stared. "Is this true?"

"It's true. I was hoping to make it a surprise...after my baptism."

"Oh, I'm surprised, Stan. I didn't think you'd actually go that far. Actually convert." Linda considered. "Then again," she said, "it makes sense. Finally, it does. You need that in your life. A movement. You always wanted to be a part of something big. Something that'll guide you. I hope it helps you."

"It will, Mom. It's already helped me so much."

Linda set her fork and knife down, folded her hands. "Aren't you going to say a prayer?"

"Not tonight. Tomorrow for sure."

I had seen my mother's eyes well up several times under this roof, but this time was different. Her tears did not fall. They gathered in her eyes like drops on a microscope slide. I watched with interest. She didn't dab at them, and they never once fell, even when she blinked and continued to stare at me. I realized then she felt pity for me. Pity—for Stan Pangborn! For the act I was about to commit? I would not be caught. She had nothing to worry about. The terrorist media would not show up at her door.

—Frank blamed her family, and later his blame centered squarely on her. His side of the family was not to blame. Those genes were unblemished, no trace of abnormality. He claimed he'd traced back to the 1500s, the Pangborn family crest, the duke and the earl, the castle and the hunt. No history of illness, only a history of perfection and renown. But Linda…. That's where the problem must have originated, somewhere down the line with the mother. A crazy aunt or grandmother at some point. And when Linda raised her fist…. The time she struck Stan in the face when he was six for back-talking. No back-talk. He knew never to do that again, ever. And when she raised her fist at other times, when she raised her fist to her husband…. She would not suffer and she would not take the fall and she would not be one of *those women*. Frank would learn. Stan had learned. Her life was not theirs, and she was glad for it.

Hours after we'd finished loading the dishwasher, Linda rose from the couch and announced she was going to bed. She kissed me on the cheek, then retreated from the living room. I watched her go, then turned to Jeri.

"She didn't kiss you good night."

"She didn't need to. That's the kind of bond we have, brother."

"I don't think so, Jeri. She didn't kiss you because she can't accept you for what you're doing. She's barely looked at you or acknowledged you're here since we got in."

—You know why that is, brother. You've always known why. Escape into your screen, escape into your church, but the fact remains—

Jeri got up from the couch and leaned toward me. I was on my phone and didn't have time to recoil. The kiss that landed on my forehead came so swiftly it was as if they'd been practicing for its delivery. I stared up, shocked. They had never kissed me before. They would never kiss me again.

"Good night, sweet prince of darkness," Jeri said.

Passing by their room that night, I felt the urge to knock. I stopped, raised my fist, dropped it. I had no reason, no reason at all. The door to my own room was also closed. I leaned against the wood and slid down to sit on the carpet. Jeri's door was in sight. I kept my eyes closed and waited.

Shepard.

"It's going to be a pain in the ass to get down."

"We'll worry about that after we eat," I said. "I have some ideas."

Jeri set their backpack down and unzipped. I watched them, tense. Before opening the backpack all the way, Jeri stopped, straightened up to their full height and turned once more to face the valley. They took a few steps toward the edge and looked down. Their back was to me.

"Now that's—"

Rushing forward, my arms outstretched, I aimed at the square of their back. My act of salvation. They would drop over a hundred feet to land on the rocks, a bloody burst of what had once been a human body. Only Stan Pangborn as witness.

An accident, officers. They got too close to the edge and it gave way. I tried to grab on to them, but we missed each other, and they fell.

We're terribly sorry for your loss, Mr. Pangborn.

Case closed.

"Jeeeeeriiiiiii!"

—

—·····—

————————

-

My hands, my fingers, lunged at a shirt, a body, and that shirt, that body, felt so real as I propelled it over the edge. As Jeri went over, their arms swung wildly, their fingers working in spasms, and for a terrifying moment I thought they would catch hold of me and drag me over. But Jeri missed. For a second they seemed to hang, seemed not to be able to fall, and then they went over, dropped (the fall, Massachusetts in the fall, waves up to their thighs Provincetown in sight, lobster on the tongue, the three-day train to New York, the four hour flight to Texas, times posted in Grand Central, skyscrapers, the towers crumbling, clutching Eric's hand afraid to fall, boating on Lake Travis, the bats under the bridge on the verge of their dusk explosion, Eric at their doorstep in forgiveness, Eric in their arms, their bed, their heart pulsing, Eric's smooth body beneath theirs on the sand of a summer's day, Eric). My brother, my sister, they. Jeri's scream will be the last sound I hear in this world.

Shrieking their name I fell on my stomach and crawled to the edge. Jeri, Jer, Jeremy, I cried out over and over. Suddenly their scream was cut short by a thud.

On the way to the Devil's Punchbowl I had prepared myself to force out tears. Now I was surprised to find that the tears needed no coaxing. I sat up and hugged my knees to my chest. They were my sibling, my twin. It was Right, but, Invincible Father, they were me.

MR. PANGBORN. Stan. Could you tell us again how it happened.

They fell. They just...fell. They were standing really close to the edge. I thought maybe they were too close. I was going to say something and then...they fell.

What were they doing that might have caused them to fall?

They were slipping. The rocks were giving way. I reached both hands out and then...

Were they suicidal at all?

No. No. Jeri was never suicidal. They—they were looking forward to their wedding.

After they fell, why did you spend so much time at the top? Why didn't you come down sooner? Didn't you think maybe there was a chance they were still alive and you could help them?

I was in shock. And I knew they were dead.

You knew.

Yes. I...felt them go. I felt them leave me, okay? I was scared. I was afraid I would fall too. I didn't want to see their body. Okay?

Thank you, Mr. Pangborn. That's all the questions we have for you.

IF THEY HAD FALLEN in the natural pool they might have lived. Though shallow it might have buffered their fall. Instead, they hit the rocks.

．　．　．

As I descended I did not look at the body. I could not. Bleeding on the boulders.

My brother my sister my brother

My self

Shrubs, sun, sky, a hawk or vulture—but no Jeri. Jer. Jeremy. I could not bear the sight of any of them.

—Jig's up, Stan. About time you acknowledged this.

"It's going to be difficult," I blubbered, for I was bawling now as I marched back along the trail. "So difficult to be without you. I've always needed you."

—What will you hate now? Oh, but you'll find something.

I ground my fists together, turned my face to the sky. "Invincible Father," I said, "Mighty, Invincible Spirit, please—"

—Come off it, Stan. Putting on the biggest act on this stage of a world.

No act, Jeri. I can for the first time in my existence say with all honesty I am for real.

—Oh yeah?

Yes. For I am the one who alone exists, and I have no one who will judge me. For many are the pleasant forms which exist in numerous sins, and inconsistencies, and disgraceful passions, and fleeting pleasures, which (men) embrace until they become sober and go up to their resting place. And they will find me there, and they will live, and they will not die again. *That's* how this ends. You'll see.

I wiped my eyes with a dusty palm. "You'll see."

Two hardcore runners, both men, both shirtless, buff, skin flushed, sweat slick on their smooth hairless skin, raced by.

They would reach the Punchbowl and Jeri's body in time for me to hear their shouts of alarm, their cries.

But as I continued, I heard nothing. Not a single human sound save for my footsteps.

When I got home, Linda asked how my hike had been. "I wish you'd gone with someone," she said.

I turned to Jeri, who had been at my side that morning, but now I stared into empty space.

I never spoke to my mother again. On the morning of Friday, July 24th, I drove my truck to San Diego International. My flight to Phoenix was scheduled for high noon. The plane arrived and departed on time.

WHEN I LANDED it was 102 degrees out and my new city, my final home, welcomed me with its dry forgiving breath. Never again would I feel a chill. I picked up my rental car as soon as I could and drove to CenterPost, the windows rolled down and my shirt sweated through. I hurried into the Center's main building, the blast of frigid air as the automatic doors slid open powerful enough to resurrect Lazarus. Two families of Manifested had gathered in the grand lobby, a wedding ceremony about to take place in one of the many halls on a floor above. For a while I watched the bride and groom, wife and husband, woman and man, soon to be happily married for all eternity, surrounded by family and friends—and so many! People are important, too. There's always somebody better. I wanted to weep at the sight of the groom who aspired to true and final manhood: godhood. I didn't deserve to be observing him as I was, from my corner in the lobby. But that was nonsense, for I would be forgiven. I too would belong to the world.

From the wedding party I turned and accosted a pair of female Manifested. "I'm here," I told the girls, "to give myself to Invincible Father. I'm here to give myself to the Church of the Manifested."

They asked me what I meant.

"I'm ready to convert. I've been through all seven of the Manly Talks, read the entire Book of the Manifested. Brannigan and Raybury will vouch for me."

Both Manifested girls looked impressed. Flanking me, they each put an arm under my own and guided me toward the stairs.

"So, you're really a Man now," one of the girls said.

"I am a Man," I said. "I want to stay a Man. I don't want to have any chance to stray. It has to be now."

THE CHLORINATED water closed over me for only a brief time, but underneath the surface I experienced tumult. A soundless rush through my ears, echo, the earliest memory. Not at all how I thought it would be. I struggled, twisted, grasped the slacks and tried to topple him, pull him under with me, but he remained steadfast. I did not want to go like this after all, Jeri, and yet I did. Many thoughts and images stalked me. The future, the mission I would complete, the Perfect I would find—may have already found—the family I would start when I returned, triumphant, to the fold. When Wheeler raised me to the surface, I stood and saw close to forty of my friends, fellow Manifested, standing poolside. The men in trunks and the girls in their bikinis. They cheered and applauded my acceptance of the one true religion. Together, on the Center's rooftop, under the savage sun, Wheeler and I reached the steps and ascended. I shook hands with all those present, and for the first time anywhere I felt I belonged. After all, I'd made these friends on my own.

WE REMAINED around the pool for a long time after, singing hymns and offering praises to Our Invincible Father. After that it would be party time, the alcohol pulsing and the nu metal cranked to the max. During the singing, however, I struggled to find my voice. Something was caught in my throat. Our hearts.

THIS MORNING I had a vision in which I find myself on a dais in a large hall with many pews and no decorations. A large pool of water lies at the base of the dais, and one after another men fall into it but do not resurface. The jumbotron screen above scrolls the names at a rapid pace. The List. The Manifest. I am in the missionary position on the dais, and I am fucking a woman who must be my wife. But as we fuck her face shifts. She is Simone. She is Erin. She is Madeline. She is crying as she speaks to me in a language I do not understand. Men surround us. They watch, their mouths and eyes open, immovable. I ignore them. I concentrate. I cannot stop, nor do I want to stop. It is, of course, the perfect sex.

About the Author

David Ewald is the author of two other works of fiction, the novel *He Who Shall Remain Shameless* and the collection *The Fallible: Stories.* He is a graduate of the College of Creative Studies at the University of California Santa Barbara and the MFA creative writing program at the University of Notre Dame. A long-time public educator, he lives with his wife and twin sons in a very flat area of California.

davidewald.net

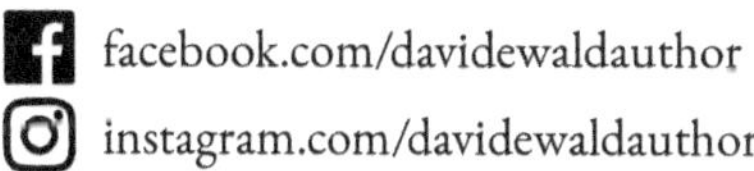
facebook.com/davidewaldauthor
instagram.com/davidewaldauthor

www.ingramcontent.com/pod-product-compliance
Lightning Source LLC
Chambersburg PA
CBHW061542310726
48972CB00008B/2572